THE
STRONGEST
Bond

FILDON PUBLISHING

Fildon Publishing
13176 S. Cherry Crest Drive
Draper, UT 84090

www.fildonpublishing.com

Book Producer: Dayna Linton, Day Agency
Editor: Anna DeStefano, Tiana Butler, Alisa Hulme, Tyson Call
Cover: Francine Platt, Eden Graphics, Inc.
Print and e-Book Interior Design: Dayna Linton, Day Agency
Photos from Shutterstock

Library of Congress Control Number: TXu00117781

Hardcover ISBN: 978-0-9987720-0-4
Paperback ISBN: 978-0-9987720-1-1
e-Book ISBN: 978-0-9987720-9-7

First Edition: 2017

10 9 8 7 6 5 4 3 2 1

Printed in the USA

DEDICATIONS

DeeJay's Dedication

To my wife of 33 years, Richelle, and our amazing children and grandchildren. The hope of our "forever family," is my greatest motivation. Also to my loving mother.

Jeremy's Dedication

To my beautiful wife, Judipa, for allowing me to pour countless hours into this book and to my two wonderful children, Lile'Ahona and Atreyu.

Special Dedication

For our friend, Grace, who beat cancer but lost her battle with the side effects at the tender age of 8. We still feel her presence.

THE STRONGEST Bond

CHAPTER 1

DEBBIE ANDERSON'S MIND AND body were overcome with a flood of conflicting emotions. The sounds of her son's end-of-the-year high school banquet echoed, amplifying her already clouded mind.

"How could it have gone by so fast?" She tussled with her thoughts. "It seems like only yesterday when Jim was my, "Little J."

She took a deep breath as her eyes wandered away from the mass of people seated around the high school gymnasium's cheaply-decorated tables. There he was—Debbie's eighteen-year-old son and only child, reanimated suddenly in the dreamscape of her mind as a bubbly, young child. Warmth and peace filled her heart as she recalled with delight the opening whistle of Little J's eight-year-old soccer season.

He had been small—very small. In fact, his lack of height had been so noticeable in the way it often had elicited muffled amusement from the opposing team's coaches and parents. The entire little league had heard the rumors about the pipsqueak on the green team.

Even at a young age, he had been said to be the best soccer player they would ever see. Although, as hard as the opposing teams tried, it was impossible for many to hide their laughter as they attempted to reconcile his reputation with what they observed on game day. Little J's X-Small shorts had covered his knobby legs like pants. However, as soon as the opening whistle had blown, the rumors had instantly solidified into gospel truth. Little J had been unbelievably fast. But more impressively, for his age he'd possessed a uniquely mature range of motion and agility.

Debbie had always loved watching Jim play soccer. However, unlike the other children his age in their community, Little J had dominated. During each and every game he'd seemed to know exactly what to do to when the ball landed at his feet. The players on the other team would try to steal the ball back, but their efforts had almost always been in vain. He had remained consistently one step ahead, dribbling past the other players as if they were standing still. Then with all the force that a child could muster, he would strike the ball, launching it straight to the back of the net.

Those games were great memories for Debbie. Watching a child succeed at something they love is the dream of every devoted mother. Although, she'd known her son was destined for something greater than merely being a soccer legend. Jim's potential had been evident to her by the miracle that had transpired at his birth. Implausibly, the young man she now sat beside at the banquet was the same child she'd nestled tightly in her trembling arms seventeen years ago. At the time, her voice had been the only tool she'd possessed as she pleaded with God to rescue the pale, near-death infant from the brink of a tragically too-short life. That night had been foreboding. But throughout those dark hours the bond between Debbie and her infant son had deepened.

"I'm trying Mom," his cry had seemed to say all those years ago. "Just hold me a little longer."

"Mom?" His deep voice whispered in the present. "You okay?"

Debbie was startled back to the reality of the banquet going on around her. Jim's sturdy hand gently nudged her shoulder.

"Wow, I was really out of it," she thought to herself.

"I'm fine, son," she said to Jim. "Is there something wrong?"

"No, nothing's wrong. Coach just gave an award to Nick. I thought you'd be excited for him. But you were just staring off in space."

"Sorry, I was just reminiscing."

Jim continued with a playful smile. "Hmmm, okay. Well, the MVP award is coming up soon. Would you please come back to earth?"

Tom, Jim's father, interrupted the conversation with a deep whisper of his own. "Son, did you prepare a speech? I don't want you bumbling around again like you did last year. That was a little embarrassing."

"Dad, come on. I don't think it's going to be me. A lot of guys really stepped up this year."

One of Jim's teammates joined in with an uncomfortably loud voice from across the table. "What? You're nuts! Who else would it be? You've been the MVP for the last three years."

A few people at the adjacent tables turned around to investigate the commotion, causing Jim's face to flush red. Debbie knew that Jim generally disliked attention. However, at just seventeen he was recognized as one of the best soccer players in the country—at any level. Magazine covers, radio interviews, and frequent news articles were a regular part of his daily life. She was always amazed that Jim tried hard to deflect much of this attention. It would have been easy for him to be like any other high school kid and bask in that kind of notoriety and gloat with arrogance. Jim's genuine attitude garnered a tremendous amount of respect and adoration from his teammates. The only Jim they had ever known had been a true team player and a great friend. However, it was clear that he had not inherited his humility from Debbie. She certainly loved a little limelight every now and then.

"Don't you think I should get a little credit if you're the MVP again?" Debbie suggested with a smile. "I'll bet it was that pink CD I made for you that made the difference."

"Your CD?" Jim rebutted before quickly lowering his head, both he and Debbie realizing that he had just barked across the table. "Mom, your CD put me to sleep," he said again with a much softer voice.

Debbie smiled.

When Jim had been fifteen and eager to obtain his driver's license, he'd never pass up the opportunity to get behind the wheel. The Anderson family tradition was that whoever drove also had control of the music. Debbie had developed the rule when Jim had been a child, to rationalize why he couldn't listen to "The Wheels on the Bus" forty times in a row. However, the once-successful strategy had backfired on Debbie, once Jim reached the driver's seat. As he grew older, his style of music had changed, but Debbie's distain for his preference had remained the same. Jim had burned a CD of vintage rock-n-roll that included the likes of Van Halen, Mötley Crüe, Styx, and Def Leopard.

He would blast the metal bands so loud that the stock speakers in their car would rattle with the strain. It was how he psyched himself up on the way to games. Debbie only tolerated the music because she knew it helped her teenage son get focused. After countless games, however, Debbie's leniency had waned. Over time, and through a lot of discussion, the two had finally reached a compromise that had been in effect ever since: Jim's CD would be their pregame soundtrack, while Debbie's would serve as the post-game wind down. With the contract in place, Debbie had burned a CD of her own. It included a relaxing mix of songs from crooners like Barry Manilow, Bread, and James Taylor. She had colored her CD with a pink marker, mostly as a joke, but also so there would be no confusion when it was her turn to control the music.

"Soccer is just a game," she would often think to herself. "Why is he always so intense about it?"

But she knew to Jim, there were no games. He treated each match as if it were a virtual trial of life or death and rarely thought about a season in its entirety. The next match had always been the thing that mattered most, and music had helped him keep his mind trained on that singular thought. The pink CD had been an attempt to bring her precious son back to reality after each match, and over time, it had grown into a token of their special relationship.

From the moment of Jim's birth, there had been a special connection between the two of them—a unique bond. Obviously, as Tiny J grew into TJ, and eventually morphed into Jim, their bond became less and less apparent to others on the outside. However, their bond remained strong, evident by the secret communication Jim had created with his mother when he was a child.

"Mom?" Little J had said years ago with apprehension.

"Yes, sweetheart?"

"I don't know what to do."

"Well, what is it that you want to do?" She had replied with the tender love of a mother.

"I want to tell you that I love you after I score a goal but," he had paused. "I don't want anyone else to know."

A deep peace and serenity had filled her heart. Debbie had been preparing herself for Little J to confess that he had broken a window or drawn a permanent marker-mural on his bedroom wall. Overcome with emotion because of her son's unique request, she had tried to hold back the tears. After a string of deep breaths and rapid blinks, she had regained her composure. Debbie had adored these moments with Little J—the small flashes in time when her little boy would approach her with deep concern over something that only a child would find problematic.

She had continued, "Here's an idea. Why don't we use a special hand sign?"

Little J had been puzzled. After a few seconds, an almost visible light bulb had lit up above his head as he belted out, "But Mom, I don't know sign language."

"You don't have to know sign language. We can just make up our own special sign, a sign that only you and I know about."

Without hesitation, he had put his hand high above his head and had made the shape of a gun with his fingers.

"How about this?" He asked, stretching out his pointer finger and thumb. "It means, 'I love you so much,' just like that book you used to read me when I was a baby."

Debbie had looked at her precious son with concern. "I don't think we should use a gun as our special symbol. What do you think? Do you think we can come up with another sign?"

Little J protested, "Mom, it's not a gun. It's half of a heart."

Debbie had been confused. She had stared at his tiny hand as he continued to point his gun in the air. She had repeated the symbol with her hand but could not understand how a gun was supposed to be half a heart. Little J must have sensed that she didn't understand because he grabbed her hand and held it up to his.

There it was!

The symbol finally made sense. Debbie hadn't noticed that Little J's tiny thumb and pointer finger were slightly rounded to create half a heart.

"This is a great sign; I love it! You are such a smart boy," she had said with a one-armed hug.

Each game since, Little J would send up the new sign multiple times—and always after a goal. As Little J grew older, this sign became frequently misinterpreted by others as some type of 21-gun salute or a victory dance. He had grown to be so associated with the "manly" symbolism of his gun salute that he had become too embarrassed to set the record straight about its true meaning.

But Debbie had known the truth and was delighted by the outward signal of their deep relationship. She was very proud of her son and knew that God had entrusted her with this child for a special purpose. She hadn't quite figured out the reason, but she hoped that knowledge would come with time.

Once again, Debbie was startled back into reality, by the applause following Coach Hobson's announcement that, "The Defensive Player of the Year is: Dave Stephenson."

The winner of the award jumped from his seat and rushed to the podium with the enthusiasm of a toddler after two hours of binging on Halloween candy. Just as Dave was about to reach the podium he tripped and fell forward. The room went awkwardly silent while a few people rose to their feet to check on his well-being. Before anyone could completely leave their seat, he jumped to his feet, held his arms high up in the air, and let out a giant, "Wahoooo!"

Coach Hobson, being not much of a comedian himself, pulled the mic back to his mouth and said, "Good thing Dave plays defense better than he can walk."

The banquet hall exploded with laughter. The boys shouted teasing jabs while parents rolled their eyes—Boys will be boys. Dave quickly dusted himself off, shook the coach's hand, and grabbed his award.

"Okay, whew. Sorry folks, I'm just a little excited," he spoke loudly into the microphone as the crowd smiled with approval. "Thanks to Coach Hobson for believing that I could play sweeper and lead the defense. Also, thanks to my teammates—you guys are awesome.

We worked so hard to be the best, and we were. We won state, baby!"

Dave held his trophy high in the air, evoking a roar of approval throughout the room. He continued to triumphantly pump his trophy up and down while obnoxiously trotting back down the aisle to his seat. As the applause faded, Coach Hobson returned to the mic.

"Folks, we have come to the last award of the evening. It has been my pleasure for the last four years to coach this young man at Owensboro High School—the finest high school in all of Kentucky. Not only is he the best soccer player I have ever seen, he's an amazing young man to boot. I have no idea what I'm going to do when he leaves for college."

"Go back to sucking," an anonymous voice shouted from the back of the room, causing half the boys to literally fall out of their chairs with laughter.

Through all of the noise, Debbie tenderly grasped Jim's hand under the table as a feeling of pride swept through her body. She had known he would win the award again, because the coach had given her a quick heads-up before the banquet.

After much effort, Coach Hobson finally quieted the room of rambunctious high school boys. "Our team captain and, for the fourth year in a row, Owensboro's most valuable player is: Jim Anderson."

The room filled with applause and everyone rose to their feet. Debbie watched her son as he hesitated a moment before humbly standing to accept the award. He turned and gave her a tight hug before holding out his hand to fist bump his dad. Their male bravado wore off quickly as Tom pulled him in close for a hug. The standing ovation continued as the father and son embraced. It was visible to all that he was excited to receive the award again. Debbie was a little worried as she knew how uncomfortable Jim was with public adulation and how much he disdained speaking in front of large groups.

After a swift slap on the back from his father, Jim approached the stage to accept the award. Coach Hobson was clearly fighting back tears of emotion as the two embraced. The coach and his star player had just finished a fun, championship-filled ride. Jim stepped up to the podium.

"Well, this is it, my last year at Owensboro—and what a year it's been. You know that I don't like, well, this speaking thing. But I do want to recognize, first and foremost, God, for blessing me with the skills to play soccer. And, um, then, of course, Coach Hobson, you're the best."

The audience politely clapped in agreement.

"Also, to the entire team, you're all MVPs."

The applause continued.

Debbie could sense by Jim's demeanor that he was feeling more comfortable.

"I especially want to thank Jake and Stan," he said. "Those two guys kept feeding me the ball in front of the net. They were like soccer chefs."

The audience let out a small, conciliatory laugh at Jim's feeble attempt at humor.

From the front of the room, Jim continued, "Dad, thanks for working your fingers to the bone so mom could stay home and raise me. Lastly, um, I want to say something about my mom. She has always been my biggest supporter and best friend."

He paused for a moment and took a deep breath, obvious to the audience that he was holding back some emotion. "Many of you know that I was very sick as a child. I had problems with my breathing. My mom used soccer as a way to get me out of the house to exercise. I think we played soccer in the backyard every day, and I don't think she ever missed a single one of my games—not a single one. She taught me to never give up. I think many of you were there, when my mom taught me that lesson."

Jim smiled before continuing.

"When I was thirteen, I wanted to stop playing for the Celtic Storm Soccer Club. I started mouthing off to the ref and other players, because I thought it would get the coach to pull me out of the game and hopefully toss me off the team. Nope, it was my mom who took that step. She literally ran out on the field in the middle of play and pulled me off. I had to sit by her the rest of the game, and the following games, until I decided to be a part of the team again. It was embarrassing, but I learned never to do that again."

Jim finished with a small laugh and the room smiled with approval as he began to choke up.

"That's my mom. She embarrassed the heck out of me sometimes, but she taught me what it meant to put others first."

Debbie looked to the front of the room where Jim was speaking, tears meandering down her cheeks.

"Mom, thanks for everything. You'll always be my hero."

CHAPTER 2

LATER THAT EVENING, SMALL groups of people were scattered around the gym discussing the night's events and reminiscing about the season. Jim had joined a few of his teammates in a corner, where they were laughing and admiring each other's awards.

"Hey Mike, did you decide to take the scholarship to North Carolina," Jim asked Owensboro's tall and athletic goalie.

"Of course, you think I could turn that down?" Mike replied.

A few congratulatory fist bumps and high-fives circled the group. Jim was happy for Mike; Jim knew how hard Mike had worked over the past few years to improve his game, and it had paid off with a scholarship offer to one of the best college soccer programs.

Mike turned to Jim. "What about you, Jim? Have you decided where you'll be playing college ball next year? You goin' to join me at UNC next year?"

"Mike, don't you follow the news?" jabbed Rob, the team's fun but loudmouthed benchwarmer. "Oh wait, of course you don't.

You're still working on the alphabet." He continued while raising his right hand and making the shape of a 'C' with his fingers. "This is a 'C;' it comes right after 'B.'"

"Yeah, and this is an 'I,'" Mike shot back, while extending his middle finger into Rob's face.

The small group erupted with laughter and a couple of friendly punches were thrown around the circle. Jim was enjoying the last formal night he would spend with his teammates. The evening was bittersweet for him. He had developed such a strong relationship with the guys on his team, but he was also ready to move to the next phase of his life.

Being the country's most impressive soccer talent, he had a hard time escaping the attention, both good and bad, that came along with that distinction. At the start of his freshman year of high school he began receiving notices from college recruiters. The following three years had become a blur as sports writers and scouts turned up at every game by the dozens.

During his junior year, a major sports magazine writer had even come to a pre-season match. She'd been so impressed by his dominance that she had penned a small article proposing that he could be the "American Pelé". But it hadn't been that comparison that had drawn the most attention—it had been the headline. She had entitled the piece, "The Savior of American Soccer," poking a little fun at Jim's dedication to his Christian faith.

That title had done it.

Once an accredited sports writer claims that someone is as good as the best historical athlete in that sport, and goes on to compare the same player to Jesus, the media hounds converge. On the sidelines of every game, reporters from all over the country had begun joining the scouts. As Jim's scoring record had increased, so had the articles and photo shoots. Scholarship offers had overflowed the Anderson home's small mailbox. One Sunday afternoon, an agent had even showed up at their house. He'd introduced himself and stated that Real Salt Lake, an American professional team, was interested in Jim making the jump onto their team straight out of high school.

Jim remembered that his mom had left him with no choice in the matter, as she closed the door before the agent could even get to the meat of his sales pitch. Jim had been set to be the first person on both sides of his family to have the opportunity to earn a college degree. His mom had always made it clear that she was determined not to let him pass up that opportunity, just to chase a few dollar signs.

Back at the banquet, Jim refocused his attention on the conversation as Mike persisted in his questioning. "Seriously Jim, where are you going to play next year?"

Jim hesitated. He knew the group was going to bash him when he announced his decision.

"It's now or never," he thought to himself.

After taking a deep breath, he said, "I've decided that I am going to play for the Purple Aces."

The group fell silent and looked at him in disbelief.

Mike questioned with a deeply condescending tone, "Dude, you could play anywhere in the country, and you picked the University of Evansville?"

"Come on Mike; it's a great school," Jim began his argument.

"Great school, yeah. But dude, their team is worse than ours here at Owensboro. Have you lost your mind?"

Jim pleaded his case. "They're getting two new assistant coaches. That's going to help a lot. Plus, it's not that far from home."

Rob laughed. "Bingo! That's it. He wants to stay close to mommy, don't you Little J?"

Jim responded with a swift but friendly punch to Rob's gut.

Rob continued unfazed. "You can punch me all you want, but you've gone all the way through high school without a girlfriend. Face it, you'll always be you're momma's Little J."

"Ooooh," the group moaned in unison at the biting insult.

"Knock it off," Jim interjected firmly.

He might be shy in public, but he was never shy with his team. He was the alpha male, and his teammates knew it.

"Look, I made a commitment, and I'm not ashamed of it. I'm not going to let you…"

Rob cut in, attempting to ease the tension. "I know, I know, Jesus boy. It was just a joke."

Jim had grown up an active Mormon, the only one in his high school, and had been consistently harassed for his unique religious beliefs. He even had a chipped tooth as evidence, courtesy of some religious-driven, freshmen hazing, when his teammates had tried to shove a beer bottle in his mouth at a party. It hadn't helped that several leaders of the local congregations in Western Kentucky had taught their members that the Mormons were evil and bent on completing the devil's work. It had always hurt and confused Jim, the anger some fellow Christians showed towards Mormons. On many doctrinal points, he had felt that their beliefs were the same. Being treated badly, however, was never going to deter him from his commitments.

Aided by the teachings of his church's youth leaders, Jim had made a conscious choice at a young age to be dedicated to his faith. He had committed to living by high moral standards—including the avoidance of alcohol, and not participating in any sexual relationships before marriage. He had been keenly aware that he was one of only a handful of high school seniors at his school that had never had sex. This greatly embarrassed him, as he hated the teasing that accompanied his stance, so he had gone to great lengths to avoid talking about the matter.

Despite the varying standards among the teammates, he knew that the banquet was supposed to be a time of celebration, not an evening of moral debate.

Jim said while putting Rob in a headlock. "You know what, Rob? Commitment this!"

After a bit of struggle, Rob eventually wiggled free and said, "You know I'm just messing with you. None of us can hold a candle to you, bro."

"I'm just messing with you too," Jim replied.

The banquet continued into the evening for another hour or so. None of the boys, especially the seniors, wanted the night to end. Around eleven o'clock, Jim and his parents finally left for home. Upon entering the house, Jim quietly made his way upstairs.

CHAPTER 3

"HE'S BEEN UP THERE a long time," Debbie thought to herself.

After the banquet, she and Tom had decided to regroup in the kitchen and wind down with some left over raspberry lemonade and double-fudge brownies that they had brought home. She glanced over at her husband and smiled. It had only taken him a couple of minutes and three of her award-winning brownies to wind down.

"So, I take it you like the brownies I made for Jim's banquet?" Debbie asked Tom with a smile.

Still with a smear of chocolate on his beard, Tom replied, "You bet I do. Doesn't this empty plate of mine tell you everything you need to know?"

Debbie laughed at her husband's sarcasm. However, her thoughts quickly returned to her concern for her son.

"Do you think Jim has gone to bed? He's been up there for a while," she asked.

"I'm not sure. You want me to go check?"

"No, it's fine. Let me run up there and see how he's doing."

She stood and walked towards the stairs before turning back to Tom and joked, "Are you going to be okay without me for bit?"

"Well, I'm not sure. I think I might starve now that all the brownies are gone," he laughed.

She smiled and headed up the stairs. Age was noticeably catching up with her. She had raised one amazing son and had just celebrated twenty years of marriage with Tom. Life hadn't always been easy. The couple had faced many financial challenges during their time together. However, their relationship had always remained strong—one of deep love and mutual respect.

Approaching Jim's bedroom door, Debbie was overcome with a warm feeling, as she thought about her son and his many accomplishments. With a soft knock, she whispered, "Jim, you awake?"

No answer.

She quietly cracked open the door and peeked inside. To her surprise, Jim was lying on his bed, staring at the ceiling with concern written all over his face. Always the overly protective mother, she slid her way into the room.

"I just wanted to say good night."

Jim maintained a blank stare.

She thought to herself, "This was such an exciting night. He should be bouncing off the walls, not lying on his back in bed."

Her concern grew as she walked closer to his bed.

"We're getting old, so I think your dad and I are going to hit the hay."

Jim remained silent.

"Is everything okay, son?"

He continued to stare into the nothingness of his ceiling.

"Okay. Well, I think I'm going to leave now. But, if you want to talk, I will…"

"No girls like me," he finally blurted out.

It took her a few seconds to understand what he had said. She was a little caught off guard by the comment. He had never been girl crazy, certainly nothing like a traditional, hormone-filled high school boy. She had always chalked that up to his intense focus on soccer.

"Oh, Jim, you know that's not true."

"No, it's true," he repeated, suddenly full of life. "I've never had a girlfriend. Not one. Not even close."

"And Dad and I count our blessings every night for that," she lightheartedly interjected, attempting to lighten the mood with a joke.

The look on Jim's face immediately let her know that she had vastly underestimated the depth of her son's feelings on the matter.

"I'm serious, mom. I love hanging out with the guys on the team, but it seems like that's all I do. There has never been a girl I've been really close to, or who has thought of me as a boyfriend. I'm so awkward around them. I mean, there are plenty who like me as a friend, but nothing more."

"I think you're being too hard on yourself. I am sure there are a lot of girls out there who would love to be your girlfriend. What have you done to let any of them know you're interested in them? You know, relationships are a two-way street."

"Mom, I've tried."

The depressed look on Jim's face was painful for her. She thought for a moment, hoping to find a way to cheer up him up. "Is there a particular girl that you have your eye on?"

"No, it's just that I wish I would have had at least one girlfriend in high school."

"Well, you need to…"

He cut her off. "I don't want to talk about this anymore. Really mom, I just want to go to bed."

"I'm just trying…"

"Seriously, mom, never mind. I shouldn't have brought it up. I just want to go to bed."

"Alright, I know you'll feel much better in the morning. I love you very much," she comforted before quietly leaving the room.

CHAPTER 4

To DEBBIE, IT SEEMED as if the summer flashed by in an instant. She hadn't been certain if she was prepared for what lay ahead. When an unusually hot July arrived, the entire state of Kentucky retreated indoors. Being constantly cooped up indoors only added to her apprehension. Jim's constant chatter about Evansville made it clear that he was ready to begin the next chapter of his life. When the day of his departure finally arrived, he systematically gathered his things and packed his bags. It took a couple of tries, and with the help of Tom, he eventually managed to cram all of his earthly possessions into the back of his worn-down car. Debbie could sense that he was ready to hit the road. However, she was not nearly ready to see him go. For her, the prior three weeks had been filled with tears and the constant drumbeat of her asking, "Can I come to Evansville with you and help you setup?"

Jim had once replied after her constant prodding, "Mom, I don't want to give my roommate the wrong impression by having you there to help me unpack. I don't want him to think I am a baby or something,"

Eventually, the small family made their way to the front porch and stood shoulder-to-shoulder. The trio remained motionless for a few moments, none of them wanting to make the departure official.

Tom finally broke the silence and put his bear claw of a hand on Jim's shoulder. "We're proud of you, son. Remember, you are an Anderson. You not only represent yourself but your family."

"C'mon Dad; I've heard the speech. How about we just stick with a hug?"

Tom put his arms around his son and the two embraced—a rare occurrence throughout Jim's young life. Jim then turned to his mother. "Mom, stop worrying about me, I'll be fine. I'm not that far away. Plus, you can call me any time."

She pleaded one last time, "I know, I know. Are you sure you'll be okay getting into the dorm by yourself? I can come with you if you want."

Tom broke in to save Jim from having to reject his mother once again. "Debbie, he'll be fine, but he needs to get going. Two-a-days start tomorrow, and he has to make a great first impression with the coach."

She finally released her stranglehold on the situation with a reluctant nod of approval. She stepped forward for one final hug—or, as she saw it, to seal the official end to Jim's childhood. She knew that he was now a man, out on his own to make a name for himself.

"I love you, son," she whispered as the moment came to a close.

"I love you too, mom," he said with his left arm still wrapped around her shoulders.

They stood in silence for a few more seconds before Jim slowly raised his right arm, adjusted his fingers into his trademark handgun salute, and fired a few shots into the air. Debbie cracked a small smile through her ongoing feelings of emptiness.

"It can't end like this," she thought to herself. "Doesn't he remember what that sign really means?"

Before she could lament any further, Jim reached forward and did something he hadn't for nearly half a decade. He deliberately bent his outstretched fingers, rounding the gun into a half heart. Her soul immediately filled with life and a jubilant burst of happiness cracked through her tear-stained face. He had not made the true sign in such a long time. The original heart that Little J had created had quickly grown into Jim's signature post-goal celebration. Often, she had wondered if he even remembered how his famous celebration had come into being. But that day she had her proof. The bond between her and her son was alive and strong.

She reached her hand up and completed the heart.

"Please never forget, son, what our sign truly means," she thought to herself. "Never forget."

After a few last moments together, Jim stuffed the last bag into the car and shifted the lever into reverse. Debbie felt Tom move in close and put his arm around her shoulders. She looked up at him and could feel that she was only seconds away from tears. With his arm around her shoulders, Tom held her tight as Jim eased his car to a stop at the end of the driveway.

"Next stop, the University of Evansville," he yelled out through the driver's side window, which was held in place by only a rubber wedge doorstop. With that, he was gone.

"I expect a call after every game," Debbie shouted to Jim who was, by that time, clearly out of range.

The car quickly turned the corner and drove out of sight.

Jim had put on a nonchalant face that morning, and it was almost starting to worry Debbie. She was feeling that Jim had no issue leaving home for the first time. With her face buried into Tom's chest, she let the water gush forth—nothing could stop the tears. Tom lovingly stood with her until she had calmed down enough to move inside.

CHAPTER 5

TOM WAS A STRONG, proud man—quiet by nature. His spirit was built like a lion, forged in the furnace of a life that had never seemed to give him a fair shake. Prior to his current position at the parts counter of the local John Deere dealership, Tom had been laid off twice in rapid succession. When he and Debbie were first married, he had been employed by a major automotive manufacturer. His clear, strategic mind and powerful work ethic had helped him quickly rise through the ranks. In short order, he had become the production manager—a position he had held for fifteen years. And then, one cool, September morning, he had been pulled into the manager's office and told that the plant would be shutting down and their work moved overseas. Unlike many of his coworkers, he had been given a relocation package. However, Tom had had other priorities and the courage to keep them. At that time, Jim had been too young and too talented to be pulled away from the only life he had ever known. With great humility, Tom had accepted a severance package and walked away.

Debbie and Jim would never understand the magnitude of this sacrifice. Tom had a stalwart character and had provided for his two dependents, even as his pride had sagged with the perceived weight of failure. He had only maintained his fortitude by knowing that he stood by his principles—family first.

It had taken three long, desperate months for Tom to secure further employment. The first position he had found had been in a coal mine. He'd hated the work but it had put food on the table. Although, after one year, the mine's production had dropped, and the company had been forced to eliminate over one hundred jobs— more than half its workforce. Even though Tom had been one of the company's most promising employees, he hadn't had union seniority. Once again, he'd had to face the difficult task of providing for his family without a steady income. The swiftness of job terminations had been enough to break any man's soul.

Without anything more than a high school education, Tom had seized any work that had come his way. Eventually, he had put to use the knowledge that he had gained from growing up on a farm. While his current job in the parts department required long hours, he appreciated the full-time employment that had allowed his wife to stay home and raise Jim. Tom took satisfaction knowing that his sacrifice had helped build the special bond between his wife and son. And this bond was all too evident in the way Debbie had reacted to Jim's departure for college.

After standing at the doorstep for what had seemed like an

eternity, Tom finally walked her into the kitchen and tenderly sat her down at one of the wooden chairs surrounding the table. A few mascara-stained tears rolled down her face. Throughout her life, Debbie had always put on a smile, but behind that mask of sunshine she had consistently battled with jealousy and insecurity. This was something Tom had learned the hard way throughout their marriage. Lately, her bouts of depression had become more frequent and harder to control. Outwardly, she was a strong woman who took great pride in her role as a wife and a mother. Tom knew that she had focused solely on Jim for the past eighteen years, and that she must be filled with fear. He was worried that Jim's absence might cause Debbie to act in ways Tom had never seen.

"Sweetheart?" He softly solicited.

"I just want to be alone," she muttered, turning her back to him.

He placed a loving hand on her shoulder.

"It will be okay. At least we'll have lots of time together now," he said.

"You have no idea. There is no way you can understand what I'm going through," she snapped, pushing his hand off her back. "Just leave me alone."

Tom flinched, not expecting the fierceness of her response. He pulled back and took a few calming breaths. Debbie's cold demeanor and stinging words hurt. She rarely behaved this way. Negative thoughts of self-doubt and loneliness crept into his mind.

"Is Jim all she cares about?" He wondered to himself.

Their formerly peaceful home was quickly turning sour around them. A stale air of anger permeated the room.

"Doesn't she know that I have feelings too?" He thought.

"You know what Debbie?" He said while turning to face her. "I have spent the last eighteen years feeling like the third wheel in this home—my home. Have you ever heard me complain? No! Not one time. The least you could do is treat me with a little respect." His large frame paused for a breath. "Well, guess what? Here's a headline for you—Tom's missing Jim just as much as Debbie. He's my son, too, you know," He finished and waited for some kind of reaction—nothing.

"I can see you're excited to spend time with me," he continued. Debbie's apparent lack of emotion only served to fuel his resentment. "Fine, just sit there. At least I will have this house to myself," he said as he stormed out of the kitchen and into his office.

Tom slammed the door with a house-shaking force.

Debbie reactively flinched and looked towards the office. The sound of silence was hard to bear. Thirty minutes passed, and they remained in their separate rooms, engulfed in their feelings of abandonment and self-pity. This moment was pivotal for the two of them. Jim was gone, and his parents were beginning a new chapter of their lives as a couple.

CHAPTER 6

DEEP INSIDE, DEBBIE KNEW her words had been wrong, and that she could not let anger win this battle. Tom was a great companion, and he had always been a loyal husband and friend, fully committed to watching over his true love. She silently rose to her feet and moved towards the office door.

"Tom?" She gently tapped on the door.

Not waiting for an answer, she slowly opened the door and peeked around the corner. Tom had folded his arms and was swiveling back and forth in his leather office chair. When she saw how badly she had hurt her husband, her pride finally broke. She had clearly underestimated the devastating power of her actions.

"Tom, I am so sorry. I really want, I mean, I really wanted to… Well, can you understand that I'm just trying to be a good mother and a good wife? I didn't mean to ignore you. Sometimes it just gets overwhelming." She paused for a response, but received only folded arms and a blank glance. "I really messed up and hurt the man who means more to me than anything," she choked through a few tears of sorrow. "I know I really messed up, and I'm sorry."

Tom remained motionless in his chair. After a few uncomfortable seconds, Debbie lowered her head and began to make her way out of the office.

Tom spun his chair around to keep Debbie's petite frame from moving towards the door. He eyed her as she reached back to pull the graceful curls of her brown hair over one shoulder. Before she could cross the threshold of the door, he said deeply from behind the desk, "You know, I could play soccer with you in the backyard now if you wanted?"

Debbie paused. Suddenly, a feeling of peace came over her as the white flag of forgiveness triumphantly waved. The look in Tom's eye's communicated that the hard shell over his heart had given way and he was ready to fill the Anderson home with love once more. She softly walked over to him, sat on his lap, and placed a tender kiss on his lips.

Debbie's soul warmed like the sun rising over the mountains on a cold winter morning.

"Wow, I'm thinking we should fight more often," he joked.

Debbie and Tom stayed by each other's side the rest of the evening, both experiencing the serenity that came from the unconditional love of your most trusted friend.

CHAPTER 7

THE DRIVE TO THE university could not have gone any slower. Jim was filled with an overwhelming nervous excitement for his new adventure. He had prepared hard for college, and it was about to begin. After what seemed like an eternity, he depressed the brake pedal and brought his car to a stop.

The University of Evansville's campus was located just north of the Ohio River on the Indiana side of the border; about a forty-five-minute drive North West of the Anderson's town of Owensboro, KY. After a couple of deep breaths, he opened his car door and grabbed a mesh bag of soccer balls from the front seat. He pulled from his pocket the campus map he'd received with his orientation packet in the mail and he quickly located the correct building. Luckily for him, he had chosen a good parking spot and his dorm was only a short walk away. Excitement turned to anxiety, which quickly gave way to a near panic attack when he arrived at the front door of the dorm complex.

"Here goes nothing," he said with a large exhale.

"Room three-twelve," Jim repeated over and over in his mind. He moved slowly down the hall, his head turning from left to right in order to examine the room number on each door.

"309...310...311...Ah, 312," he whispered.

Jim dropped the bag of soccer balls and pulled the room key out of his pocket. A bead of sweat rolled down his left temple.

"I hope my new roommate likes me," he thought to himself.

Hopes, doubts, dreams, and anxieties flooded his mind. For a moment, he remained frozen with fear. After a few short breaths, he wrangled enough courage to maneuver the key into the lock. Slowly turning the handle, he pushed the door open and peeked his head around the corner. The room was precisely as he had imagined—a rectangle area with just enough space for two small beds, two desks, and a TV tucked against the back wall. Jim's side of the room was completely empty. The other side was covered with dirty clothes, pictures of the world's best soccer players, and a couple posters of girls who were covered with only a few strategically placed strings that he guessed could have classified as swimsuits. Suddenly, he realized that his new roommate was lying on the bed, head cocked back and upside down, looking right at him.

"Um, hey, I'm Jim," he said. "I guess we must be roommates."

"Jim, huh?" Said his new roommate, spinning around and propping himself up on the bed. "Didn't know I was getting a new roommate today."

"Oh, yeah, just drove in this morning."

"So, you a soccer player?"

"Yeah, I'm joining the team this year."

"I know," his new roommate said with a bit of sarcasm. "I'm Lance," he said while holding out his hand.

Jim stepped forward and shook his hand.

"Dude, what am I, your dad? I don't want to shake your hand, help me off the bed."

Jim flushed with embarrassment and reached forward again. He locked hands with his new roommate and pulled him to his feet. Instinctively, he put his hand out for a second time, eager for a proper introduction.

"Hi, I'm Jim Anderson," he said, hoping that the intro would go much better the second time.

"I know who you are," Lance laughed while slapping Jim's hand away. Jim was confused.

"How do…how do you know who I am?"

"Are you serious? Everyone on the team knows who you are. You're the superstar rookie. You're LeBron James. You're Derrick Jeter. You're the "American Pelé", remember?"

Jim shrank with embarrassment and tried to change the subject. "So, are you on the team too?"

"No," Lance retorted while letting the 'O' hang, to emphasize his sarcasm. "Dude, you're a real piece of work aren't yah? Coach asked me to keep an eye on you this season, so you better be worth it. I was going to move off campus for my senior year, but now Coach has me babysitting you instead."

Lance bent down and opened a small fridge under his bed, grabbed a sports drink, and flung it in Jim's direction. With only milliseconds to react, Jim caught the flying projectile with his free hand before it struck him directly in the groin.

"Hey, you really are a superstar," Lance laughed. "You know what? I'm going to give you a pass today. I have an entire year of hazing planned for all of you cocky freshman, but today I'll let it slide. Think of it as a welcome-to-the-neighborhood gift."

Jim smiled. "Sounds good to me."

"Why don't you throw your stuff on the bed and let's head down to The Union. Freshmen move-in-day is the absolute best time to check out the ladies. Young, vulnerable, home-sick girls looking for a little comfort. It's like a buffet from hot chick heaven."

"Um, maybe another time. I have a lot of stuff to do before classes start on Monday."

"Are you kidding me? C'mon, I need to show you the real reason you left home for college."

Lance forcefully pushed Jim out the door, putting an arm around his shoulder. "Practice starts tomorrow, and this is our last day of freedom. Get your butt out the door, and let's get moving. So many ladies, so little time."

CHAPTER 8

FOR LANCE, THE FIRST practice was a prime opportunity to show the incoming freshmen players his comedy routines. He had built a monumental reputation for interrupting every practice with a barrage of jokes. His favorite, although it was never funny, was to recreate Allen Iverson's famous rant, "Practice? We talkin' about practice?"

"You ready for the first practice?" Bryant hesitantly asked Lance as they made their way from the locker room to the field.

"Practice? We talkin' about..." Lance began his routine, right on queue.

"Hey," Bryant interrupted while shoving a hand in Lance's face. "Seriously, you're going to pull that crap again this year? Coach about ran us to death last year because of your stup..."

"We're not talkin' about a game," Lance pressed on, unfazed by Bryant's plea.

All the veteran players knew exactly why Bryant was nervous

about the first practice. Coach Peterson was notorious for his intense training camps. He would run his players to the brink of collapse, and the next day, he'd make them to do it again.

"What's up with that guy?" Adriel, the team's captain the prior season, interjected as he and the other players arrived at the field.

Near the far goal, a lone player had roughly twenty soccer balls lined up at his feet. He was rhythmically launching each one of them into the corner of the goal from about thirty yards out. Lance was impressed, but there was no chance he was going to acknowledge it. Instead, he and the rest of the guys stood resolute, skeptical of the lone shooter's presence.

"That's him," Lance said. "That's my shadow."

"What's he doing, trying to impress us?" Adriel replied while taking off his shirt. "He's got nothing on me. This is how you do it boys."

Adriel crunched his stomach and pulled his arms into the standard flex—revealing a magazine-worthy physique. He was a six-foot-two hunk of muscle from Chicago and was never afraid to display that he had a body that would put half the magazine models to shame. He also never passed up an opportunity to use his physique to gain instant respect from his peers. Adriel was a senior and expected to continue his leadership role on the team this year. He pulled a ball out of his bag and dropped it at his feet. He took a couple of steps back and launched the ball in the direction of the lone player. The ball curved slowly to the left, crossing forty yards of grass and open air before whizzing only inches past Jim's left ear.

"Dude, what are you doing?" Lance yelled while shoving Adriel.

"That rookie's okay, man. Definitely not good with the ladies, but he's alright."

"No wonder Coach put you in the same room. Nothing like a couple of cupcakes," Adriel laughed and took off towards Jim with Lance chasing close behind.

Lance would have typically loved to participate in the hazing he knew Adriel was about to deliver. However, he thought Jim was alright, and that maybe the team could spare him some humiliation on the first day

"Hey Rook, see them bags?" Adriel said while pointing over to the bench. "New guy carries the bags. Mine goes over there by the bench. I mean, your new home for the season."

Puzzled, Jim looked over at Lance.

Though he felt for his new friend, Lance knew that Adriel was right about the unwritten rule—rookies carried the bags.

"Sucks to be the new guy," Lance said and shrugged his shoulders towards Jim.

He could see that Jim was uncomfortable and a little shaken by this situation. He felt a small ping of compassion. However, he quietly swashed it and ran to catch up with Adriel and the rest of the guys.

CHAPTER 9

JIM HAD ALWAYS BEEN the undisputed leader on every team he had ever joined. This situation was different. Confusion quickly turned into shameful obedience. Jim picked up Adriel's bag and reluctantly carried it to the sideline. Shortly afterwards, the coach arrived and practice began.

About an hour into the training session, sweat was dripping off each player's face as the Indiana sun beat down and the humidity stuck. Coach Peterson, in typical fashion, was holding nothing back. He was frustrated, and Jim could sense it.

"Come on!" He screamed. "You guys got soft over the summer. Let's pick it up. We're not going to finish in the bottom of the pack again this year."

Easy passes were sailing far overhead and shots were landing nowhere near the goal. Water breaks seem to be the only thing the team cared about. Every player was dogging it, except one. Jim was outrunning them all. After yet another unapproved water break,

Coach Peterson commanded his team to line up for a new set of drills.

"Jim, you're up first," he called out.

Jim, already having a ball at his feet, headed straight up field. The drill began and Jim effortlessly passed the first defender. He glanced up and saw Lance running down the left side of the field. Lance was calling for the ball by pointing to the near side of the goal box. In full stride, Jim gently chipped the ball over the last two defenders, who could do nothing but watch as Lance ran past them to arrive in unison with the ball.

The pass from Jim was perfect.

Lance had headed a ball into the goal hundreds of times, but never before from such a perfect pass. For a split second, he was almost sad he was in the middle of the play, because it would have been fun to watch. With a quick flick of his neck, he drove the ball past the goalie and into the back of the net, before landing in perfect stride with all the gusto of a professional soccer star. Lance took off his shirt and waved it in the air, making sure that everyone within a two-hundred-yard radius was aware of his accomplishment. He ran around the field waiting for the standard congratulatory pile of people to overwhelm him, but it never came. Nobody moved. Somewhere between utter exhaustion and the shock of the most perfect pass any of them had ever seen, everyone was too overwhelmed to respond.

Lance ran by Jim with his arms still raised in celebration. "Nice pass, Rookie!"

"Nice header, Roomie," Jim cheered loudly in response.

That did it. An avalanche of laughter overcame the speechless shock on the field.

"Dude, did you just call me, 'Roomie?' If that pass hadn't been so amazing, I would kick your butt right here, right now."

"Hey, Honey Bun," Adriel interjected from a few yards off. "Or, maybe we really should call you Cupcake?"

"Good one, Adriel," Lance responded with deep sarcasm. "Actually, you know what, Cupcake is already taken. Or, at least that's what your mom calls me."

After a good laugh and a couple of playful shoves, the team settled down and finished the drill. Another water break ensued, and Coach Peterson decided to end the practice with a scrimmage. Fifteen minutes into play, the scrimmage became intense. However, the concentration was not enough for Coach Peterson. He called the team to the sidelines and announced that any player he caught dogging it would be finding a new home warming the bench, every position was up for grabs. The threat sent a tremor across the field. Veteran players did not want to lose their positions, and the underclassman saw it as a golden opportunity to earn starting positions on the field. The scrimmage intensified to the point that tempers were flaring—exactly what Coach Peterson had intended for his first day's practice.

With only minutes left in the scrimmage, Jim won possession of the ball. He bolted past one player, then a second, and then a third. He looked up at the goal and thought about launching a shot from thirty yards out. However, at that exact moment, he eyed a fellow freshman named Carson streaking down the left sideline. Jim quickly decided that passing the ball wide was the better option. In less than a second, the ball was in the air and heading towards Carson, who was sprinting with every ounce of strength left in his exhausted legs. The ball landed only a couple of inches from his feet, allowing him to receive the ball in stride and head straight towards the opposing goal. Although the pass was nearly perfect, Carson didn't have the skills to move past the last defender.

"Cross center-front," Jim yelled over to Carson.

Carson looked up and once again tried to shake the defender but couldn't. The easy scoring opportunity was lost as Adriel quickly recovered and began tightly guarding Jim. Eventually, Carson got some open space and gained control of the ball. He passed it backwards to Bryant. Bryant struck the ball high into the air. Adriel moved between Jim and the goal. The ball was rapidly approaching, but in Jim's mind, time seemed to slow while he determined the best move.

He turned and faced the ball flying towards him, leaving Adriel guarding tight on his back. The ball slammed into Jim's chest and he expertly directed it towards his left foot. He contorted his upper body, legs, and feet with one continuous motion in order to open a yard of space between him and Adriel. Jim moved past Adriel with such speed and skill that Adriel became so off balance that he fell to the ground with an embarrassing thud. He had no time to recover. All he could do was look up from the grass as Jim struck the ball past the outstretched arms of the goalie and into the corner of the net.

Jim raised his hands in jubilation and ran toward the center line of the field. Lance ran over to Adriel, still prostrate on the ground, and stood over him.

"Who's carrying your bags now?" Lance declared, his statement oozing with sarcasm before he tapped Adriel's head with the toe of his cleat.

Adriel punched the ground, clearly embarrassed. With their formerly undisputed captain on the ground, Lance ran over to Jim and laughed, "Hey, maybe you are the American Pelé."

CHAPTER 10

LANCE WAS BECOMING IMPATIENT.

"Dude, let's go!" He called out. "Bryant's downstairs and he's blowing up my phone."

"Okay, I'm just finishing up my hair," Jim said. "Give me a sec."

"Bro, what are you so worried about?" Lance asked. "You're not going to attract anything with your stupid country-boy haircut anyway. Put down the comb, and let's roll."

With one last, careful stroke of his hair, Jim replied, "Alright, I'm set."

They grabbed their backpacks and rushed out the door.

"Why are we going to class so early?"

"You just don't have a clue do you, Superstar?" Lance said while stopping in the stairway to confront his questioner. "This isn't about grades, man. It's about the law of the jungle. You know what the law of the jungle is, don't you?"

"Umm, I think so," Jim replied.

"It's survival of the fittest," Lance shouted through the stairwell. "Check this logic: Humans are just like animals, right?"

"Yeah, I suppose."

"Okay, so that Darwill or Drake guy, whatever his name was, said that chicks dig the strongest and fastest dudes, right?"

"You mean Darwin? Well, I guess that might be true, but..."

"Jim," Lance cut him off. "I can tell you just don't get it. Listen to me. Ugly dudes get chicks all the time. See, Jim, you think like some brainiac scientist, and they don't understand either. They're all stuck in their scientific method and quantum physics and stuff. You've got to mix everything together, like a stew or one of those Jell-O salads you're always talking about. Think about it. What do all the business professors say about business?"

Lance looked at Jim and received only a blank stare in return.

"Location, location, location!" He yelled, grabbing Jim's shoulder for attention and shaking him with each word. "It's all about location, and I've got it all figured out. For the entire year, everyone sits in the same seat they sat in during the first day of class. If we go early, we can scout out the hot girls and make sure we sit right by them. This guarantees us first dibs the entire semester, with the best-looking chicks."

Lance paused, waiting for Jim to respond.

"Okay, I think I get it," Jim said, finally breaking the silence.

"Finally, I was beginning to think you know nothing about women."

Lance was satisfied that he had pulled Jim aboard with his plan, and the two rushed out the front door to meet Bryant in the parking lot.

CHAPTER 11

JIM HAD NO IDEA what Lance had meant with his rant, but he had no intention of asking more questions. He knew Lance had been talking about girls, the one area in Jim's life that he had yet to conquer.

"Room CR201," Jim said while opening the door to the classroom. Both Lance and Bryant had to retake a few of the classes they'd failed as freshmen, and they had procrastinated long enough that now during their senior year, the three teammates were now in Economics 101 together. Luckily for Lance and Bryant, economics was one of Jim's favorite subjects.

Unfortunately for Jim, Bryant was also quite the lady's man and immediately began his coaching tips as soon as they entered the room. "The trick is to scope out the girls you want to take to your room an—"

Lance swiftly jabbed Bryant in the side, stopping him from making his inevitably crude comment. Bryant winced with pain and shot a look at Lance.

There seemed to be an unspoken communication between the two before Bryant continued, "The girls you want to "hang-out" with during the semester."

Lance nodded in acceptance of Bryant's modified comment, while the group turned to survey the room. The large, open space had stadium-style seating that angled downward towards where the professor would stand.

"Definitely not in high school anymore," Jim thought to himself.

"Come on," Lance instructed while pulling Jim to the right side of the room. "I've found the herd. Let's get into position."

The trio moved down to a row of seats roughly thirty feet from the lecture podium and situated themselves in front of four attractive girls. Jim nervously placed his backpack on the tiny fold-out desk attached to his chair. Anxiously he slid into his seat. However, his right leg bumped the edge of the desk and knocked his backpack to the floor. The heavy books landed on the tiled floor with an echo that crisscrossed throughout the entire room. A hundred gazes shot his way, and the muffled laughter from the group of girls behind him caused his face to flush. All he could do at that point was humbly pick up his bag and slide deep into his chair.

"Smooth move, Superstar," Bryant whispered while easily taking his seat, leaving an empty space between them.

It also seemed that the bang had garnered the attention of the professor, who had previously been writing on the whiteboard with his back to the students.

"Ah, a nice, grand entrance for our newest soccer sensation."

The room erupted with laughter.

Professor Thompson was notorious for being one of the school's most boring professors. His thick British accent did little to counter the impression. The unlikely prospect of Professor Thompson actually telling a successful joke made his attempt seem twice as funny. Soccer had never been a hugely popular sport for the Evansville student body, but Jim was such a high-profile recruit that he had garnered a lot of attention from the local papers.

Twenty minutes into the class, Jim felt a bit more relaxed. With the professor well into his lecture, Jim gathered enough courage to take a quick glance at the tempting pair of tan legs he'd glimpsed stretched out behind him. He gently swiveled his torso, positioning his head towards the clock on the wall, with his eyes gliding in the opposite direction. He caught sight of smooth skin extending from a frilly white skirt.

There was something incredibly intoxicating about the tiny goose bumps covering her thighs. He didn't know how long he'd been staring at those legs when their proud owner caught him in his drool-producing trance and returned his smile. In a panic, he quickly shot his attention to the clock on the back wall. He tried to pull the, "I'm just looking around the room," act. But he was busted, and he knew it.

When the professor eventually diverted Jim's attention back to the whiteboard, the girl with the legs made her move. She quietly slid out of her chair, down one row, and slipped into the open seat between Bryant and Jim.

Nerves ripped through Jim's body, and his hands clammed up.

She had total control over the situation and he knew it. As she settled into her new seat, she looked directly at Jim and nodded her head to the side, as if she'd suddenly recognized Jim from somewhere. She paused for a moment before reaching into her bag and pulling out the campus newspaper. Sure enough, it included a story about Jim and his decision to play for Evansville. The article was titled, 'The Freshman Phenom,' and included a large color photo. She put the paper on her desk and motioned for him to look in her direction.

Until that point Jim hadn't seen the article. And now that he had, he just about died on the spot. A week earlier, the newspaper had called him about writing an article on his perplexing decision to attend Evansville. They had asked if he could provide a photo for them to use with the story. He'd been busy and mostly uninterested, so he had asked his mom if she could take care of it for him. He had assumed she would send one of the many action shots she had taken over the years. However, Debbie, who thought his high school senior class photo was cute, had sent them an 8x10 of the shot. And there it was, for the entire campus to enjoy.

She leaned over and asked, "This you?"

Jim felt ill. Not only did he lack the social skills to handle the situation, he now had the attention of female perfection focused in his direction. "Uh, I think so."

"So you're that good, and you chose Evansville? That's interesting, don't you think?"

On the soccer field, Jim had an answer for every move, every strategy. At that moment, however, he felt hopelessly lost in a torrent of nerves and lust.

"Can't speak?" She asked while moving very close to Jim's ear. "Am I making you nervous?"

The soft puffs of air from each syllable tingled his ear and shot fire through his limbs.

"You know," she softly teased, brushing his ear with her bottom lip before backing away with a seductive, and somewhat sinister smile. "I've got a quiet place we can go if you want to get out of here,"

Jim was frozen with fear as she leaned back into her chair. The smirk on her face sent signals that she was enjoying every second of Jim's reaction.

Over the next ten minutes, Jim tried to regain his wits by staring straight ahead.

Lance on the other hand was doing all he could to make things worse. He sent winks and blew mocking kisses in Jim's direction. Shortly after taking his seat, Lance had informed Jim and Bryant that he had chosen to sit amongst a pack of freshman girls. He'd made it clear that he had no interest in anyone in that age group. His tastes were a little more experienced.

Jim could sense by her anxious movements next to him that she was developing a new plan. His intuition was confirmed when she quickly moved back to her seat behind Jim. She gently slipped off her heels and crossed her legs. Each time the professor looked away, she would gently touch Jim's neck with her toes.

Jim was mesmerized; his attention was understandably on something other than the economies of scale discussion going on around him. However, as much as he loved her warm touch on the back of his neck, he knew it had to stop. He was in college to get an education, and he was serious about it.

"Cut it out," he quietly commanded.

"Something wrong?" She smirked.

He wasn't sure how to react. Instantly, two voices appeared in his subconscious. One of the voices reminded him to stand firm in his principles, and the other oozed with the fun of carnal endeavors. The whole situation was becoming too much for him.

Without any forethought, he turned his entire body around and loudly snapped, "Stop it!"

His abrupt yelp woke the rest of the students in the room from their semi-comatose state. Stopping mid-sentence, Professor Thompson moved directly in front of Jim. From first grade through high school, Jim had taken pride in the fact that he never made trouble in class. In fact, he was considered somewhat of a teacher's pet.

"Well, Mr. Anderson," the professor said. "It seems like all you want to do is disrupt my class."

Jim's mind went blank. He lowered his head and looked at the floor, floundering to find a rebuttal. "Well, I was just…"

Professor Thompson continued, "We've all seen your larger-than-life picture in the school paper. Being an athlete does not give you a pass in my class."

"But…"

"Mr. Anderson," Professor Thompson cut him off. "You can wait for me in my office to discuss your continued participation in this course."

"Yes sir," Jim respectfully answered.

"Well, go ahead. Pick up your belongings, get out of here, and meet me in my office immediately after class."

Jim could hardly breathe; he felt as if he was going to pass out with embarrassment.

"Ha! Even I wasn't kicked out of class on my first day," Lance teased with a laugh as Jim gathered his things to leave.

"I'm Sydney, by the way," Jim heard whispered into his ear before turning to see Sydney lean back into her chair with an accomplished smile.

Jim was filled with embarrassment and dropped his head as he walked across the front of the class to the exit. As he pushed the door open he couldn't resist looking back at her. But to his surprise, her sinister smile was gone and her expression contained a glint of remorse.

"She's a jerk," Jim said to himself and shook his head to remove that final image from his mind.

CHAPTER 12

JIM WASN'T EXCITED TO go to practice. He was emotionally exhausted and was not excited that Coach Peterson had decided to start that day's practice at four in the afternoon – in the hot sun.

Typically, the guys would casually drift onto the field at their leisure before warm-ups. Jim was one of the last to arrive. For most of the players, practice was just that—practice. However, something about the way Jim played each day made his teammates marvel at how much he loved the game. But today, Jim couldn't seem to match his teammates' enthusiasm. After the incident in class, he was visibly down. The lingering embarrassment and guilt from that morning had failed to diminish, and Jim's day was about to get worse.

After a couple of hours, Coach Peterson gave two loud blows of the whistle to end practice. The team congregated at the center of the field for final instruction and the traditional team cheer.

"Bring it in fellas. Great practice today; we are starting to look like an actual soccer team," said Coach Peterson. "I don't know what they were thinking in the Athletic Director's Office, setting us up with the University of Indiana as the opening game. But, that's the task at hand, boys. We've got to stay focused, if we're going to have any shot at beating those guys."

Coach Peterson paused, and a serious expression came over his face. He steadfastly directed his attention towards his team. "Professor Thompson called me this afternoon."

Jim froze.

"He told me about an incident in class with one of my players," Coach said with a look that Jim felt pierce deeply into his soul.

He tried to sink his head in shame, hoping that this was only a dream. Getting in trouble was not something that he ever did. Every muscle in his face tensed up with an attempt to keep the water that was welling up in the corner of his eyes from streaming down his cheeks.

"Jim—you have anything you'd like to say to the team?"

Jim could feel everyone dart their attention towards him. The look in their eye's was clear—they were in disbelief that the culprit was the straight-A, Mormon kid with the country boy haircut. Lance, probably. But, Jim? No way. The look on Coach Peterson's face was clear—this was no joke. The new rookie had been busted on the first week of practice. Jim looked ahead in silence, frozen with fear. He had never found himself in this type of a situation before, and he hadn't the slightest clue how to respond.

Coach Peterson finally broke the silence. "You know my policy. I will not allow behavior like this in our program. At this school, men's soccer has to scrape for every bit of funding it can get, and I will not tolerate any bad press with the administration. With that said, I ensured Professor Thompson that I'd take care of the problem tonight at practice."

The coach moved directly in front of Jim, "You are going to stay for an extra hour of conditioning—nonstop conditioning. Do you understand?"

Jim nodded his head in confirmation, eyes full of water and face flushed red.

"If this happens again, your spot on the team will be on very soft ground."

The whole situation was just too much to handle. An unwanted tear finally broke free and ran down Jim's cheek. "Yes sir, this will never happen again."

The rest of the team broke from the huddle without a cheer.

For most of them, Jim's rebuking was uncomfortable and kind of embarrassing. Their superstar had just been broken right in front of their very eyes.

CHAPTER 13

LANCE DARTED HIS ATTENTION towards Jim in disbelief.

"Yes sir, this will never happen again," Jim replied.

Lance felt genuinely sorry for his roommate, whose eyes were now red, a single tear rolling down his cheek as he took off on his extra conditioning run. Lance might be the model of a care-free, California boy, but Jim was now his brother-in-arms. Lance also knew Jim loved soccer more than life, and that he had more humility than anyone on the field. Suddenly, a feeling of brotherly love overcame Lance, and he knew what he had to do. He immediately dropped his bags and sprinted towards his guilty teammate. Working hard to catch up, Lance finally pulled alongside Jim.

"Thought you could use a chaperone," Lance said. "I've seen you firsthand with the ladies, and I don't want you alone by yourself after dark."

Jim cracked a smile.

"Hey," Lance reassured, "keep your head up. I've got your back this season."

Matching stride for stride, the two jogged around the field.

As they finished their first lap, Lance looked over at Adriel and motioned for him to join them. Adriel looked at him with searching eyes, apparently battling internal emotion about whether to join or not. His decision became clear when he turned and walked towards the locker room.

After Coach Peterson's hour-long punishment, Lance and Jim hit the showers before limping back to their dorm room. Lance threw his bag on the desk, jumped on his cheap, squeaky mattress, and fiddled with the remote. Jim quietly placed his gear in the closet and sat down at his desk. He reached for his calculus textbook and cracked it open. Lance hardly took notice of Jim's motion, having found a special pre-season football rankings show. Lance had to know where his hometown UCLA Bruins were going to land in the polls.

"Can you believe that? Seventeenth? No way. There is no way UCLA is…" Lance carried on with his hysterical rant. "Hey Jim, can you believe what that guy just said? He has no idea…"

Lance turned around to see why Jim wasn't as upset as he was.

"What are you doing?" He asked. "You missed the entire segment on the Bruins with your face stuck in that book."

Lance could not have known, but there was no studying going on. Jim was simply putting on a facade to hide his feelings of regret, and the fact that his legs were burning from the punishment. After a brief moment of silence, Jim responded with a soft but contemplative voice. "Hey Lance, thanks for today."

"No problem. I need to get you in shape anyways. You look soft out there on the field sometimes."

"No. I mean, thanks for being my friend."

"Um, okay. Why don't you just get back to your book?" Lance responded with an uneasy, confused tone.

A pinch of awkwardness filled the room, so Lance turned up the volume to fill the void.

As much as Lance was a jokester on the outside, he was a man of high character in his heart. His good looks and fast wit helped him get where he needed to in life. He had always been a popular guy; the guy that everyone had wanted to hang with at parties. Nonetheless, when Jim had called Lance a friend, it had secretly filled him with a kind of inner peace. But, for as long as he could remember, he had always felt a deep loneliness inside. People always seemed to want to be his friend because he was funny, and not because they genuinely liked him. With Jim, something was different. Lance had felt himself developing a true friendship for the first time.

"Let's go get some pizza," he later proposed. "It's Ladies Night at Turoni's."

"Nah, I need to finish this homework and then call home."

"C'mon. We're talking about pizza, chicas calientes, first class, royal…"

"Seriously, you go ahead. I'll catch up with you in a half hour."

"Alright, suit yourself. Just don't do anything I wouldn't do."

"So, I can pretty much do whatever I want?" Jim retorted.

Lance smiled. "Lame attempt at humor; but I'll give you a "B-" for effort."

Jim smiled. "I'll take it. It's better than any grade you'll ever get."

"That's the spirit, Rookie. Now you're gettin' it." He laughed and opened the door to leave the room.

Jim quietly returned back to his desk and picked up the phone.

Lance walked down the dorm hallway but stopped a few feet short of the stairs. He continued to feel bad for Jim and wanted him to be happy. He instinctively turned and jogged back to the room. As he approached he could here that Jim had put his mom on speaker phone, so he stopped short of the door and listened.

"Jim, I've missed you so much," Debbie said

"Mom, it's only been a day since we last talked."

"I know, but I've missed you this whole day," she said. "Hey, I have some big news. I got a job today. I'll be working for Dr. Borgen as his receptionist."

"That's great, Mom," he sluggishly replied. It was obvious to Lance that Jim was still down.

"Well, I didn't expect you to do cartwheels or anything, but I thought you'd at least pretend to be excited for me. I quit work when you were a baby to stay home with you. Now I'm back at it."

"It's not that, Mom. It's just been a really bad day."

"Oh, son, I'm sorry. What happened?"

"Well, it all started in econ," Jim began. "I thought teasing stopped when you left high school, but I think I was wrong."

CHAPTER 14

TWO DAYS LATER, SYDNEY found herself once again on her way to economics.

She hadn't been able to get Jim off her mind, and she wasn't entirely certain why. She had every intention of doing anything she could to ensure that they sat by each other again. As she approached the class door, she decided to hang back about twenty feet and keep her head down in an effort to hide her presence. Just as class was about to begin, she finally noticed Jim approaching the backdoor to class. It was apparent that he was trying to sneak in. However, Lance came running up directly behind him.

"Ready for another fun day in biology?" Lance asked; startling Jim, whose cover was now blown.

"Ah, you do know this is econ, right?" Jim replied.

"Econ, biology, what's the difference? I never bring my books anyways," Lance said.

"Well actually, Professor Thompson said that we needed to

complete our..."

"Blah, blah, blah. Let's go sit by those girls again and get back at them. I got your back this time, bro."

"I think I'm going to sit over there," Jim hesitantly replied while Lance was pushing him into the room.

Sydney waited a couple of more seconds before she quietly entered the room through the back door. She quickly spotted Jim, but there were no open chairs around him, so she had to settle for a chair on the other side of the room. As she passed in front of Jim, she looked directly at him, but his focus remained immediately at the professor.

She felt a feeling of anger rise inside her. It has been a long time since she had been rejected this badly by anyone.

From the moment she sat down, she kept watching Jim, hoping to catch his attention. She really wanted to continue with her escapade from the previous class. She had a reputation to maintain, and Jim had been just the latest in a long list of fall-guys. However, as the class progressed, she couldn't get him to look her way. He maintained an intense focus on the lecture.

"Does he really care that much about school?" She thought.

A strange sense of guilt began to creep into her stomach. Maybe she had done more than just mess around with this guy; maybe he had been truly humiliated? She had assumed that Jim was just another jerk like most of the other athletes on campus.

"Why did I pop that guy?" She reflected, regret beginning to brew.

Sydney was an experienced flirt, and this was certainly not her first time around the block. She had tagged guys all the time in high school: leading them on, and then dumping them when they had run out of money or had wanted a deeper relationship. However, something was definitely different this time. All throughout high school, Sydney had been at the top of the social food chain. Although she had been very intelligent, she had chosen to focus on her skin-deep talents. She was very beautiful and certainly not the type of girl Jim would have had the courage to ever approach on his own.

She worked hard to maintain a trendy hybrid of class and edge. Flowing, jet-black hair hung just past her shoulders. Her full lips were consistently stained red with bright lipstick, and she maintained her makeup at a near-professional level. Two dangling earrings accented her beautiful face, and the small tattoo on her left hand added some intrigue. The result was a look that was simply stunning. She was accustomed to using these looks to gain social status. From early on in her life, to everyone around her she had seemed to be the most beautiful, popular, and important girl. So far, Evansville hadn't been any different. She had known she could attract any guy she wanted, because she always had. However, Jim had posed a challenge to her reputation.

Sydney's inner reflections were abruptly interrupted by her friend, Ashley, who asked, "Why do you keep looking over at that nerd? Haven't you had your fill of him? You need more?"

"No, no, I'm just…"

In reality, Sydney couldn't stop herself from looking over at Jim for the entire ninety-minute class. Each time she glanced in his direction, a feeling of uneasiness pinged her soul.

It was all too obvious that Jim made a conscious effort not to look at her. He may have seen her with his peripheral vision, but he'd never made eye contact. As soon as the bell rang to end the class, he rushed out the door, leaving Sydney alone to her thoughts.

CHAPTER 15

THAT YEAR HAD BEEN unusually hot, and the temperatures that day were projected to break records. Coach Peterson briefly considered cancelling the practice but quickly squashed the idea. The thought of playing at Indiana weighted heavily on his mind. The coaches' pre-season poll had ranked the University of Indiana as the third best team in the county. Coach Peterson wanted to use every minute he could get to prepare his team. The athletic trainer had set up on each sideline two sprinklers and drinking hoses, in an attempt to keep the players cool. After assessing the situation, Coach Peterson decided it would be best to simply lead an inter-squad scrimmage to keep his boy's thoughts off the heat.

CHAPTER 16

DURING THE SAME TIME as practice, Sydney was just finishing her last class of the day. Biology had only been offered that semester as an afternoon class, so she didn't finish until four. As the class came to an end, she headed out the door and began walking down the sidewalk toward her apartment, located just on the edge of campus. Strangely, she had not been able to get Jim out of her mind. She couldn't understand why she cared so much. Even worse, she could not stop her legs from moving her towards the soccer field.

"Maybe if I just apologize, this will all go away?" She reasoned with herself.

The concept of apologizing seemed absurd. She honestly could not remember the last time she'd ever felt the need to apologize for anything. But the incident with Jim was really bothering her, and she wanted those feeling to stop. Whatever drastic measures had to be taken, she was ready to take them.

She walked down the hill to the lower portion of campus, a route that would take her a significant distance from her apartment. However, she was motivated and needed the feeling to go away. Sweat began to build on her brow. The heat was relentless. A tiny drop rolled down her spine, following the contours of the exposed skin on her lower back. Finally, the soccer field came into view, and she was in luck. The team was still heavily into their practice. Nerves shot through her body as she moved down the path, until she reached the fence surrounding the field. Pausing for a moment, she looked for Jim but couldn't see him. She took a few more steps down the sidewalk to get a better view.

There he was.

By the time Sydney had reached the field, the entire team had their shirts off and had sweat pouring off their bodies—the sun was unrelenting. Jim was on the opposite side of the field, too far away for her to get his attention. Sydney had never been much of a sports fan and had never actually watched anyone play soccer. In high school, as a cheerleader she had only attended football and basketball games. She watched for a few minutes, but the game was inconsequential to her; she was completely focused on Jim.

"That can't be the same guy from class?" She thought.

Jim's moves on the soccer field were powerful and dramatic. His tan, athletic body moved seamlessly in concert with the ball. Coach Peterson blew the whistle for a brief water break, and the entire team moved in Sydney's direction. They gathered at the water fountain about twenty yards away from her. Jim's body glistened with sweat. With each swig of water, his abs flexed, ripping tight with lean muscle. His thighs were thick and tensed with strength at each step. Sydney hadn't the slightest idea how soccer was played, but it was easily observable that everything Jim did was smooth. He was unquestionably more stunning than the other players on the field.

After the water break, the team ran back onto the field to resume practice.

"Wow, he's amazing," she mouthed to herself after watching Jim sprint down the field calling for a pass.

He leaped into the air and struck the ball with his left foot into the goal.

"He's like a ninja," she joked and smiled to herself. She clapped with excitement, and a smile gleaned across her face, revealing her stunning white teeth. Jim celebrated the goal with his teammates by exchanging a barrage of high fives. Tingles ran down her arms, and her heart was racing. After the excitement of the goal, he took a moment to catch his breath while looking around the field. Sydney began nervously playing with her hair, not knowing if she wanted him to spot her. As Jim looked in her direction, she felt that she had lost control of the situation. Instinctively, she gave a little wave and pressed her beautiful smile into a suggestive pout. He didn't seem to notice.

"Did he just ignore me?" She wondered.

Pride took over. Now she had to get his attention. She gracefully rose up on her toes and called out, "Jim!"

He didn't respond, so she made a second attempt. This time, once again, her effort was met with failure. Embarrassment took hold, and it suddenly seemed a better idea to make a quick exit.

CHAPTER 17

"YEAH, I SEE YOU," Jim thought as he followed Sydney out of the corner of his eye.

Truthfully, he'd seen her from the very beginning. The entire team had. How could they not? She was the definition of physical perfection. But, Jim knew her heart. He had made a conscious effort to stay focused on the game and avoid any type of contact with her. She had embarrassed him enough for a lifetime, and he wasn't going to give her that kind of power again. He could only imagine that she was at the field that afternoon for a little more fun at his expense. She may have been the queen of the classroom, but the soccer field was his kingdom, and no one was going to take that away.

The whistle blew and Coach Peterson called everyone to the center of the field. He waited for the team to quiet down and catch their breath.

"Tomorrow, we leave for Indiana. I don't have to tell you how tough it will be. They've won their conference title for three years in a row and have beaten us every time that we've played." Coach Peterson paused and looked around at the players, "Until this year!"

The team erupted with excitement.

"If we are going to make it to the tourney this year," he continued, "we will have to beat those guys. Stay focused and don't be late for the bus." Coach Peterson paused again and surveyed his team. "Bring it in."

Jim put his hand in the circle. "Evansville!"

He quickly looked back over to where Sydney had been, but she was gone.

"Good riddance," he said to himself.

CHAPTER 18

THE UNIVERSITY OF INDIANA, a school that had recruited Jim heavily in high school, was the preseason favorite to win their Conference: The Big Ten. The Hoosier soccer team was the talk of the region and had a genuine shot at making a national title run. Jim had made two recruiting trips to their campus, but the thought of living that far away from home had swayed his decision. Even the enticement of a full-ride scholarship hadn't broken his resolve. He'd rejected their offer.

Evansville's bland, gray team bus pulled into the parking lot next to the soccer field. This was it; the first game of the season. Coach Peterson was the first to step off the bus, followed by the players in single file. An Indiana school official arrived shortly and directed the team to their locker room. Coach Peterson took up temporary residence in a small office behind the last bank of lockers. After placing his computer bag on the desk, the coach took a few minutes to relax and quietly reflect on the events that were about to transpire. Before

Jim had become part of the team, this type of game meant one thing only for Evansville—money. It was customary for larger schools to schedule smaller schools as their first opponent of the season. They would use those less talented schools as their "final practice", and as a check in the win column to kick off the season. In return, the smaller university was able to limp home with a loss and the much needed capital to keep its program funded for another year.

Jim, however, had done something to the Evansville team. Coach Peterson hadn't quite yet figured out what that meant, but he was hoping to soon find out. After a few moments, a soft knock came from the closed office door. Jim was looking at him through the adjacent window.

"Coach, can I talk to you for a minute?"

"Sure, come on in, son."

"Would you mind if I played a pump-up CD in the locker room while we get dressed for the game? It's kind of a superstition thing for me."

"Well, I don't think that would be a problem. What kind of music is it?"

"Old rock-n-roll; you know, the kind of stuff from your day—seventies rock."

"My day, huh?" Coach said with a smile.

"Well, I didn't mean it like that, It's, um…" Jim fumbled around.

"Because I'm old, is that it?" Coach barked with a smile. "That's fine; just make sure you turn it up, so old people like me can hear."

They shared a laugh as Jim exited the office. Coach Peterson leaned back in his chair and let out a short exhale.

"It's hope!" The thought suddenly ripped across the Coach's mind. "I've got hope!"

Jim had given the entire team hope—Coach Peterson could finally see it. The Evansville team had a long history of mediocrity, and they had the culture to match. During his short tenure with the school, Coach Peterson had done a lot to change that precedent. But there had only been so much he could do without wins to back up his dreams.

After coaching a mediocre team for a few years, a new sense of hope was refreshing. He had only felt this type of preseason excitement once before: during his playing days, when his team had made a deep playoff run. And now he knew something extraordinary was about to happen this year. Jim seemed to play with a higher purpose. Most of the team's athletes had been lured to Evansville with the promise of a scholarship and the ability to play soccer for a few of more years before having to grow up and find a steady occupation. But Jim was fundamentally different. He played with a passion that infected everyone around him.

Nerves were high in the locker room as the Evansville players dressed for the game. The only sound in the air was the click of cleats on the tile floor. However, Jim had a smile plastered across his face and couldn't wait to get the team pumped up for the game. He reached into his bag and pulled out his well-used rock CD. With sequenced clicks on the floor, he walked over to a dusty boom box that sat in the corner of the room, on top of the bank of lockers. He opened the plastic case, placed the CD in, and pushed play. The opening riff to a classic seventies rock song blasted from the speakers.

This song was Jim's favorite.

He slowly turned the volume knob to the right, causing the famous guitar riff to scream off the metal lockers. Coach Peterson stood up at the sound of music and looked out his window into the locker room. Every other player also looked up, a, "What the heck is Jim doing?" expression crossing each of their faces.

With each strum of the bass, the metal lockers vibrated. Jim was sitting on the bench tapping his foot and bobbing his head to the music. His right hand was moving rhythmically, as if he were stroking a guitar. When the chorus began, he cranked up the volume as loud as it would go and jumped up on the bench.

"What are you doing?" Someone screamed over the music.

"Getting pumped!"

Almost as if on cue, Bryant, wearing nothing but his briefs, hopped onto the bench and threw a pair of rock horns high into the air.

"Of course he would do that," Coach Peterson laughed to himself, knowing that Bryant never passed on an opportunity to goof off.

In the Indiana locker room, the team was loose—they knew the purpose of this game. However, they still had something to prove. All week long, their student newspaper had published articles; not about them, but about the American Pelé. The Indiana players wanted to prove the newspapers wrong and were determined to show the world that Jim was just another overrated freshman. However, the pounding drums and singing coming from the Evansville locker room was unsettling. Indiana had never heard an opposing team so loud before a game, especially a warm-up game like this. Unknowingly, the seed of fear had been planted in the back of the Indiana player's minds, and that was all Jim would need.

Coach Peterson exited his office and yelled to the players, "Out on the field fellas; it's game time!" He paused for a second. "And Bryant, put your shorts on. You've certainly got nothing to brag about."

The room erupted with laughter while Bryant stood with a look of shock plastered on his face. His famous quick wit failed him.

"Game on!" Jim yelled to the group.

The team burst out of the locker room and ran out onto the field. Coach Peterson knew they were jacked up.

CHAPTER 19

PLAYERS WERE SICK OF warming up, playing against one another, and they were eager for the game to begin. The ref put the whistle to his lips.

"And so it begins," Lance said to Jim. "My last season; let's make it count."

Jim pushed the ball forward to Lance, who was waiting to his right. The first game of the season had begun.

From the very start, Evansville was sharp with their passes. Adrenaline flowed and their minds were focused. The Evansville players moved quickly to open spots on the field, causing Indiana to fall behind on every pass. Indiana hadn't prepared themselves for this competitive of a game. Each time an Indiana player made a good play on the ball, Evansville seemed to counter with three plays of their own. Surprised and frustrated by Evansville's discipline, the Indiana players began to scream at one another—vile language spewing across the field. During a stoppage of play, roughly ten minutes into the game,

Jim ran up to Bryant on the right side of the field.

"Their left-D can't match your speed. I'll draw the sweep with the ball. Once he commits, break for the goal. I'll strike it far side." Jim finished his instructions by pushing Bryant back into play.

The ball was thrown in and Evansville's defense quickly won possession. Jim ran back across the midline and received the ball at his feet. He deliberately positioned himself in the center of the field and saw the opening he had been waiting for. With only two defensive players to beat, Jim took off up the field like a rocket, blowing past the first defender.

"One man to beat."

He looked to his right and saw Bryant, as instructed, breaking away from his defender. With no time to think, Jim struck the ball and sent it flying off his left foot. The spin was extraordinary and caused the ball the curve beautifully through the air. The pass was perfect. Bryant was certainly not the best player on the field, but he was lightning fast. He quickly gained two yards on his defender as he blazed towards the ball's ultimate destination. The goalie began to inch forward while Indiana's defense, in a panic, raced towards their goal. Their effort was too late, leaving their goalie hung out to dry. Jim watched Bryant look up to spot the ball sailing through the air and then down towards the goalie that was charging his way. With a short mental calculation, Bryant captured the ball at his foot and directed his entire soul through to his leg. The ball whizzed past the goalie, through the posts, and snapped into the back of the net.

Bryant's enthusiasm could not be contained. He ran to the left side of the goal box, fell to his knees, threw his hands high in the air, and let out a triumphant scream. One by one, the team piled on top of him to celebrate. Coach Peterson jumped to his feet and hugged his two assistants. The Indiana crowd sat in a stunned silence. Eventually, with the help of the ref, the Evansville boys began to disperse, and both teams jogged back to their sides to continue the game.

Over the next fifteen minutes, the speed of play intensified, and Indiana's coach grew visibly furious. His nationally ranked team was being outplayed by the "warm-up" team. Evansville was keeping the heat cranked up high, holding the ball almost exclusively on Indiana's side of the field. They continually fired shots on the goal. At one point, an Evansville player took a shot that had the speed of a bullet. Indiana's goalie barely got a hand on the ball, diverting it around the goal and out of bounds. Indiana's coach had had enough; he was done with Jim taking over the game. The coach jumped to his feet in an attempt to sway the refs in his favor.

"Come on, ref. He's pushing off; this is a joke," he screamed across the field.

The ref looked over at the coach but chose to ignore the outburst.

Lance ran to retrieve the ball and placed it on the corner of the field for the kick. Setting up the play, he gestured to his teammates by putting his right arm high in the air. With his signal, the Evansville players darted into motion. Jim jetted into position from just outside the goal box, to the near side of the goal. Lance struck the ball low and hard. In full stride, Jim stretched out his leg and gracefully touched the ball to the lower corner of the near post. The handful of Evansville spectators screamed with excitement as Jim crashed to the ground. Unbelievably, the ball flew inside the post and into the goal.

Evansville was now up two-to-zero.

Jim made his way to the center of the field with a couple fist bumps, flashing his trademark sign along the way. The Indiana players looked confused and deflated. Their heads hung low in disbelief. Coach Peterson was running up and down the sideline throwing high fives to anyone within reach, and screaming, "We're taking it to them! We're taking it to them!"

The mood on the field became electric with the realization that Evansville actually had a chance to beat Indiana. With the first half coming to a close, the Indiana players were becoming more frustrated and angry. Silly mistakes were made—something not typical of a championship caliber squad. Then, in an instant, another scoring opportunity for Evansville materialized. The ball was passed to Jim a few feet outside Indiana's goal box. Once again, he easily beat his defender. From fifteen-yards out, Jim cocked his leg back to strike. Trying to recover, the Indiana defenseman lunged forward and caught Jim's leg from behind, forcing the ref to make the easy call. Evansville was awarded a penalty kick.

"What? Are you giving them the game?" The Indiana coach screamed while running deep onto the field. "How can you give them a penalty kick right before half?"

On the Evansville side, Coach Peterson seemed relaxed, sitting on the bench enjoying the other coach's furious tantrum. A few of Evansville players were milling around the ball that had been placed on the penalty kick spot, twelve yards directly in front of the Indiana goal. During the entire delay, Jim had been standing bent over with his hands on his knees.

He motioned to Adriel. "You take the shot."

"You took the fall; it's your shot," Adriel replied.

"I can't. I'm still feeling that one."

Adriel didn't put up too much of a protest. He bent over and repositioned the ball on the torn grass for the penalty kick.

"Jim, I want you to take the shot," Coach Peterson shouted across the field.

Jim had moved outside the goal box and was, once again, slumped over with his hands on his knees, ignoring the coach's instructions. He was laser focused, staring straight at Adriel. However, he could see out of the corner of his eye that Coach Peterson was franticly trying to get his attention.

"Jim! Jim! I want you to take the shot! Jim!"

Frustrated with the fuss the coach was making, Jim looked over to the sideline and intentionally waved off the coach's instructions. Jim could see by the stern look on his coach's face that he was not happy about his orders being disobeyed; a transgression that Jim knew was not tolerated.

However, the veteran coach soon relented, sending the unspoken message that he knew Jim was establishing himself as the leader on the field. Evansville had an opportunity to beat one of the best college teams in the nation, and Jim was demonstrating leadership way beyond his years. The decision was easy–play on.

"Hit it clean, Adriel," Coach Peterson yelled from the sideline.

The ref signaled for the shot with a blow of his whistle. Indiana's goalie stretched his arms out wide, palms forward. He was rocking back and forth, ready to leap right or left. Adriel took a deep breath, exhaled forcefully, and took a few steps forward to strike the ball. The goalie took a chance and dove to the right—he guessed wrong. To ensure that he wouldn't miss right or left, Adriel kicked the ball directly into the middle of the goal. The ball easily rolled into the net for the score.

Evansville—Three; Indiana—Zero.

"Nice shot, Adriel," Jim yelled with excitement.

"That don't make us even, Rookie," Adriel coldly replied.

Moments later, the referee blew his whistle and pointed to the center circle; half time.

CHAPTER 20

INSIDE THE EVANSVILLE LOCKER room, the players could hardly contain their excitement. Wild cheers and high fives filled the room.

"Okay guys, let's not get too excited," Coach Peterson tried to direct his team over the hoots and hollers. "We still have another half to play."

There wasn't an ear in the room listening to a word he said. Across the hall, the mood was vastly different. One by one, the Indiana players trudged in, plopped themselves down onto their benches, and hung their heads in defeat.

"This is pathetic!" Their coach roared, slamming his way through the door. "You're getting beat to the ball, and they're controlling the middle. I won't even bring up our defense. You guys look like you've never played the game before."

He stared directly at his central defender. "You afraid of getting your uniform dirty?" No response. The player cowered with fear, and he wasn't the only one. The entire team dared not look directly at their coach. "Second half, we're making some changes. I want players out there who haven't quit and aren't scared to shake it up. Everyone else stay on the bench."

The coach entered his office and slammed the door in disgust. Indiana's somber mood soon turned into anger as they tried to grasp onto something to change the momentum.

CHAPTER 21

A S THE TEAMS ENTERED the field for the second half of play, the prior sold-out crowd had dwindled to only a smattering of loyal spectators. It seemed as if the Indiana fans had no desire to watch their team lose to the no-name university from down the road.

"Let's just get through the second half with no injuries, okay?" Coach Peterson said to Jim as they trotted out to the field.

"No worries, Coach," Jim responded with the carefree spirit of a child.

"Play smart, Jim. I know we are up right now, but don't forget we still have an entire season left to play. I'm going to need you."

With the blow of the whistle, Indiana shot out of the gate with a renewed level of intensity, swarming to the ball and tackling hard. Jim immediately recognized that the second half was going to be much different than the whipping Evansville doled out during the first. A few minutes into the half, Bryant was awarded a corner kick. He jogged over to the corner while an Indiana player marked Jim tightly in front of the net. The defender was grabbing Jim's jersey and throwing in a few sharp elbows, just for good measure. Clearly, Indiana's new strategy was to take Jim out of the game with dirty play. Unfortunately for them, Jim was no rookie when it came to playing against a frustrated and angry opponent. Situations like this had occurred consistently throughout his life of soccer.

"Don't take that from fourteen," Lance said to Jim.

"Thanks, mom," Jim replied with a sarcastic smile.

"I'm not kidding, bro. If you're not going to man up, I will. We may never be the best team in the region. But we have a reputation for being tough, and I'm not going to let that change."

"Come on, I can handle myself. Just focus on winning the game," Jim instructed.

"Dude, you play for Evansville—we don't take that crap."

Jim moved to the top of Indiana's goal box with his defender shadowing close. As Bryant set up the ball for the corner kick, Jim and the defender began pushing, grabbing, and jockeying for position.

"That's it," Lance yelled with disgust.

Like a pit bull protecting his turf, Lance ran over to the pair. He forcefully lunged toward the defender and knocked him off balance with a powerful, two-hand shove to the chest.

"Lance, not like this," Jim yelled, trying to get Lance under control. "We don't need a red card. Let's not finish this game a man down."

Lance roared back, "You may be a wimp; but I won't let Evansville get slapped around."

"Not this way, Lance. Not this way," Jim shouted while Lance turned and walked away.

The referee had watched the entire scene play out. He immediately ran over and flashed a yellow card directly above Lance's head.

"Lucky you didn't get a red," Jim barked. "Come on man, settle done. Let's just finish this game, get the win, and go home."

Obviously still hot, Lance waved Jim off and ran a few yards away to prep for the corner kick.

"Let me show him how it's done," Jim mouthed to himself while watching Lance move to his position.

Jim knew exactly how to play the game, and Lance was about the get an education from the young master teacher. With play resuming, Bryant sent the corner kick high into the air towards Jim and his defender. Like a gazelle, Jim leapt into the air, high above the Indiana player. He flicked his head to the side, striking the ball towards the goal. However, his shot on goal was the least of his concerns at that moment. As both players collided in midair, Jim swung his bent arm forward and struck the defender's mouth with a cheap and vicious elbow. Both players fell to the ground while the goalie easily caught the ball with his hands. Blood began to pool on the grass under the Indiana player who remained on his stomach while Jim immediately popped up to his feet. He looked down at the whimpering mass—blood oozing out of a split lip.

"Number thirteen, come here," the ref screamed at Jim after blowing his whistle.

"I'm sorry, ref. I caught him with an accidental elbow. It was an accident," Jim pleaded.

"I should give you a card for that one."

"I know; I definitely hit him. But it was an accident. I swear it was an accident. I didn't mean to hit him."

Soccer is as much an art as it is a sport, and Jim was a thespian for the ages. The referee took the bait and kept the card in his pocket. As the trainers ran onto the field, Jim walked over to Lance and gave him a sinister wink and a nod. "Now that's how you do it."

"Did you just pop that guy intentionally?" Lance asked with a laughed. "I didn't think you had that in you."

"Well, maybe I do have a few tricks up my sleeve," Jim winked and ran back to his position.

CHAPTER 22

THE HIGH INTENSITY PLAY continued for the last thirty minutes of the game. No additional goals were scored before the final whistle blew. The Evansville coaches and players stormed the field to congratulate one another. They had beaten one of the best teams in the country, and the celebration was going to last well into the night. In the locker room, Adriel sat down on the bench for a much needed rest. His uniform was soaking with sweat; he'd left everything he had on the field. Looking up after a few, exhausted breaths, he glanced to the corner where he eyed Jim quietly kneeling in a corner offering a prayer.

Adriel had grown up in a very rough environment on the streets of Chicago. He'd been raised in a single mother home, and throughout his young life he'd never had any sort of male role model to guide him. His dedicated, loving mother had worked two jobs to make certain her son had the opportunity to get the best education possible and break the heavy chains of poverty. She had worked six days a week, sometimes more than fourteen hours a day. With Sunday being her only day off, she would attend church when she had the strength.

She had been a deeply spiritual person and educated her son early about her beliefs. However, as Adriel had grown up, his faith had never strengthened, eventually dwindling away in apathy. He had questioned God as a young man and had serious doubts by the time he was a teenager. Watching his mother work her fingers to the bone while she consistently thanked God and considered herself blessed had left a confused and bitter taste in his mouth.

Adriel had been a good soccer player, but scholarship offers hadn't come his way. The only one he had received had been from Coach Peterson. The coach had attended a tournament in Chicago where Adriel first caught his eye. Looking past some of Adriel's weaker soccer skills, Coach Peterson had focused on Adriel's lightning speed and physical strength. On-the-spot he had offered him a full ride scholarship. Understandably, Adriel had not been excited to live in a small town in the middle of nowhere. His mother, however, had been overjoyed. Her dreams of having a son earn a college degree and find a way out of the inner city had come to fruition.

The main problem for Adriel during his first three years at Evansville had been that he never really assimilated to life in the country. Out of respect, he had put on a good face around his mom and had worked hard to get good grades, but he rarely socialized outside of the soccer team and mainly kept to himself. He had always carried a heavy chip on his shoulder, knowing that many of his teammates hadn't a clue about what he had faced as a teenager growing up in the city. Jim was certainly no exception.

"What a punk," Adriel thought as he looked over at his teammate whose head was still bowed in prayer.

"Gather 'round boys," Coach Peterson yelled, breaking up Adriel's train of thought.

The team scuttled to arrange a few benches in a U-shape and gathered in front of their coach.

"In the past, my postgame speech after Indiana has been about recovering from a loss; but not tonight!" He screamed while pumping his fist in the air. "I'm so proud of all of you. All I want to say is that we are on our way to Evansville's first ever division title."

The team exploded in a carnival-like frenzy. The festivities, high fives, and chest bumps took a while to calm down enough for players to shower and dress.

Adriel watched Jim, Lance and the rest of the team bounce around the locker room with excitement.

"Enjoy it Jim. But just remember, this is my team," Adriel mouthed to himself.

CHAPTER 23

"JIM, WHERE DO YOU want to celebrate tonight?" Lance questioned as they left the locker room following the game.

"I think I'm just going to stay in the hotel."

"What? Not a chance; we just beat Indiana. It's time to party."

"Really, Lance. I need to call home, and I am swamped with homework. I just can't."

"C'mon, man," Lance tried again with frustration in his voice.

"Seriously, this is the first game my mom has ever missed in my life. I'm not kidding. I bet she's sitting by the phone dying to hear how the game went."

"There's no way calling your mom is your excuse."

"I'm serious. I really need to call home."

"Okay, suit yourself country boy. That just leaves more of Indiana's finest for me."

CHAPTER 24

THE FOLLOWING MONDAY, THE energy on the Evansville campus was high. The news of the soccer team's imposing win had spread across the country. The University of Evansville was now on the map. A highlight clip of Jim's first goal made ESPN's top-ten, and articles littered the regional newspapers. Player's faces were uncharacteristically recognized around campus. The soccer team was out of obscurity, and all of the players gleefully strutted around campus like they ran the place. Suddenly, everyone wanted to know about the, "Stormin' Mormon," and his band of flying, "Purple Aces."

Even Coach Peterson couldn't recall a time when a college soccer team had received this type of overnight exposure. Typically, just to get a lowly intro-to-journalism student to write a story about the team, he'd have to apply exasperating levels of pressure to the University's Communication Department. On the Monday after the Indiana game, however, the team had earned notoriety, press, and swagger—lots of it.

Sydney had also succumbed to the frenzy. She'd woken before sunrise, just to ensure that she would be able to snag a copy of the student newspaper. After quickly gathering her things, she'd rushed to the student union to find a newspaper box. She had timed it perfectly. By the time she arrived, the student delivering the papers had just started placing the first stack into the box. She quickly approached the paperboy and peeked over his shoulder. The upper half of the folded paper contained a large headline—"Kings of Indiana"—and a color photo of Jim. She was anxious to grab a copy, and the paper boy could sense it.

"It's just the student paper," he mumbled with a heavy, sarcastic tone. "No Pulitzer in here, you know."

"Very funny," she popped back, swiping the top paper off the stack he was holding.

She immediately unfolded the paper and examined the large action shot of Jim on the front page. He was jumping high in the air, challenging his opponent for the ball. She couldn't understand why, but she was infatuated by this guy. Sydney thumbed through the paper looking for articles about the team. Truthfully, she had very little interest in the details of the game. She was hoping to find more pictures of Jim.

CHAPTER 25

WHEN THE NEXT GAME rolled around, it seemed as if the entire Evansville student body wanted to attend. Sydney was no exception. She nudged her roommate Ashley towards the massive crowd that had gathered around the soccer field.

"C'mon, Ash; we need to get in line," she said.

"Sydney, are you serious? Are you positive you want to spend a Friday night at a soccer game? Do you even know how soccer is played?" Ashley replied while unbuckling her seat belt and sliding out of the car. She was trying to keep up with Sydney's rapid pace.

"No; but I'm sure we can figure it out. We need to show some more school spirit anyways."

Ashley stopped before passing the end of the car and looked stubbornly at Sydney. "I hope this isn't because you tagged that nerdy Mormon kid from class. You know Mormons don't drink or smoke or have any kind of fun whatsoever. You don't actually think a guy like that is going to like a girl like you, do you? There's no way…"

"Ash, this isn't because of that guy. I'm just trying to turn a new leaf this year, and I think we need to participate in more school stuff," she lied.

CHAPTER 26

THE EVANSVILLE SOCCER TEAM was determined to prove that the Indiana game was not a fluke. Their intensity and concentration was at an all-time high. Within a matter of weeks, Jim had instilled in his team a culture of hard work and professionalism. The players were ready for the next game and were resolute in their determination to win. However, when the next game arrived, they weren't prepared for what awaited them off the field. As the team exited the locker room, the swarm of people waiting in line outside the chain link fence determined to get seats for the game was overwhelming. The raucous crowd had grown so immense it extended into the parking lot for at least a hundred yards.

The stadium, although small when compared to the many college football stadiums around the nation, was one of the finest locations dedicated specifically for soccer. The bright green patch of grass was surrounded by a chain link fence and had a section of bleachers and a score box on one side of the field. Players from both teams occupied the other side of the field, sitting on weathered metal benches placed on opposite ends of the midfield line.

The size of the crowd attempting to enter the field was obviously going to overwhelm the spectator bleachers. Historically, only a couple hundred people would attend a home game, the majority of those being family and friends. However, thirty minutes before the start of that day's game, the crowd had already grown into the thousands. The largest past crowd anyone on the team could remember had been five or six hundred people, for a grudge match against Evansville's top rival. After Evansville lost that game, the crowds had dwindled back to normal.

Seattle Pacific, Evansville's opponent for this home game, was also nationally ranked and had climbed the polls to the number eight spot. Like Evansville, they had dominated the previous week, with a score of six-to-two. Their striker, Raul Gutierrez, was the pre-season favorite to be the NCAA player-of-the-year. The previous year their goalie, Josh Taylor, had been conference player-of-the-year. Seattle Pacific had scheduled Evansville two years prior, believing that the game would be an easy, out-of-conference win. They could never have foreseen a player like Jim choosing to play at Evansville.

Jim was more than a little overwhelmed by the amount of people streaming in the front gates. He had played in front of scouts and college coaches for many years, but he had never played in front of a home crowd this substantial. Jim tried to remain focused during the pregame warm-ups, but he could not keep his eyes from searching the overflowing bleachers for his parents. As hard as he searched, he could not find them. Debbie had told him that they were going to come early to the game so that they could get front row seats. However, with all the people standing in front of the bleachers, trying to cram their way up the stairs, he couldn't see the first few rows.

Suddenly, Jim heard the loud, screeching whistle, and he knew that screech all too well. His eyes darted to the stands and immediately spotted his mother at the top of the bleachers, waving her hands for the entire world to see. He quickly returned the salutation with a wave of his own. Debbie pointed down to the front of the bleachers, pointing out where she and his dad were sitting. Jim laughed as he imagined what he knew had happened—his mother fighting her way to the top of the bleachers just to get his attention. He loved that about her; she would do anything for him.

Jim tried to refocus on the pregame warm-ups, but was having trouble. When he looked over at Bryant, it seemed that he was also having trouble focusing as well.

"Can you believe how many people are here," Bryant shouted with a smile towards Jim and Lance. He rose from his leg stretches and jogged over towards the pair. "My brothers, I can't focus. Have you ever seen this many ladies in once place before?"

"No way. I guess winning a big game brings out the masses." Lance said. "Everyone's jumping on the bandwagon."

"I'm okay with it," Bryant said with a smile. "I'm heading over there. I've got to cash in on this fame. You guys want in?"

"No buddy, it's all you," Lance laughed.

Bryant turned and jogged toward the crowd. Jim's eye's followed as Bryant made his way to the bleachers; where he fortuitously spotted Sydney making her way from the entrance to the overflowing bleachers. She was absolutely stunning—a living, breathing portrait of perfection. Her hair shimmered in the glow of the florescent lights. There was something incredibly intoxicating about her. She was everything Jim was not. And, yet, he was pulled in her direction. He attempted to remind himself about the episode in class, but his pounding heart was winning out.

"I've got to stay focused," he thought, literally shaking his head to keep thoughts of her from overpowering his will to play.

When it was time, the teams quickly organized on opposing sides of the field, and the whistle blew to start the game. It became apparent that the blowout win at Indiana was no fluke. Jim and his team had so much swagger that night, even a major league team would have had a difficult time putting a shot on the goal. Only minutes into the game, Jim rocketed a shot into the back of the net, surprising even himself with the ease of his goal. The already standing crowd jumped and cheered with excitement while Jim gave a couple of gun shots into the air.

Jim ran towards his mother, whom he could see was going wild with excitement.

"Game on Jim! Show 'em who's boss!" She screamed to Jim as he ran by. The game wore on, and the momentum never shifted. Evansville dominated play from start to finish. Seattle Pacific had no hope, and Jim knew it. At that moment, he looked up at the clock.

"Five minutes to go," he said to himself.

His mind was slowly losing focus on the game, while random thoughts of Sydney fluttered in to fill the space. He looked over again to where she was sitting. Unlike the rest of the standing-room-only assemblage, she had skillfully flirted her way into the middle of a group of guys on the front row. Jim focused in on her dark skin and her beautiful curves—she was inebriating. His heart raced out of control—a similar rush as to when he is streaking down the sideline for a shot on goal. A sudden and overwhelming urge to show off took hold of his mind. He looked back up at the clock and surveyed the score.

Evansville—Four, Visitor—Zero.

"We got this," he reassured himself while consciously deciding that Sydney was now more interesting than the game going on around him.

Jim reengaged in the game, eying for an opening where he could direct the ball to the crowd's side of the field. Lucky for him, that chance came less than a minute later. An opposing player had gained control of the ball and was casually moving it up the sideline. Jim took off in a full sprint for twenty-five yards, before aggressively sliding into the Seattle Pacific player. He expertly knocked the ball away, popped to his feet, and gained control.

"Jim, what are you doing?" Coach Peterson screamed from the sidelines.

To any outside observer, it was seem bizarre to be making such a strong tackle with the game well in hand. But Jim knew exactly what he was doing. He immediately took off up the sideline to position himself in front of Sydney.

"What is he doing?" Lance stared in disbelief.

When Jim arrived close to where Sydney was sitting, he slowed to allow a defending Seattle player to close in. His plan was setting up perfectly. He pushed the ball forward then raced as fast as he could to get in front of Sydney, attempting to time the convergence of all three—the opponent, the ball, and himself. He looked to his left and made eye contact with his opponent. At that very instant of distraction, he made his move. With a quick movement of his feet, he stepped in front of the ball and stopped the momentum on a dime. The opposing player slid, in an attempt to knock the ball away, but he was too early. The defender could have never imagined that someone would have had the ability to stop so rapidly. Sydney jumped from her seat, as the opposing player went sliding into the front row of the bleachers almost careening into her and Ashley. Jim calmly looked over to the pair and gave a little wink before booting the ball up the field.

Lance watched the entire event unfold. He may have been pretty good at soccer, but he was an expert in the flirting arena.

"Dude, did you just peacock?" He laughed.

"Yes, I think I just did," Jim responded with a smirk plastering his entire face.

Jim regained his position, allowing time for his adrenaline to fade.

"What am I doing?" He questioned himself. "I hate that girl."

CHAPTER 27

S YDNEY LEFT HER SEAT in the stands with about one minute re-
maining in the game. She wanted to beat the rush out of the
soccer stadium, to ensure that she would be outside the locker room
before Jim left. The night was incredibly hot and muggy, but that was
not going to stop her. She had to talk to Jim. Her determination was
strong to apologize and to get the nagging feeling out of her stomach.

She waited for over an hour on a cement planter box outside of
the building that housed the locker room. Sports were hardly her
expertise, and she had greatly miscalculated the amount of time it
would take for Jim to complete his post-game meetings and shower.
However, just as an inkling of doubt crept into her mind, the doors
leading out of the locker room swung open with a loud bang, and
the team began to file out of the building. She quickly jumped to her
feet with nervous energy pulsating through her veins. About fifteen
guys had exited the doorway before Jim finally appeared, walking
between Lance and Bryant. Her heart skipped a beat, as she took a

deep breath to steady her thoughts.

She looked directly at Jim. It seemed like he was intentionally diverting his attention in the other direction, but eventually they made eye contact. Sydney motioned for him to come over to her, but he just seemed to stand there. She thought it was weird but she was determined to give her apology, so she walked over towards Jim. He never moved, only stared at her. His awkwardness was actually quite unnerving, even for a dating-veteran like Sydney. She had been so used to frat boys with premeditated pickup lines and smooth talk, that Jim's radiating apprehension filled her with anxiety.

"Hey, can I talk to you for a sec?" She asked.

CHAPTER 28

JIM EXITED THE LOCKER room flanked on each side by Bryant and Lance. The second he walked out the door, he spotted Sydney out of the corner of his eye. He tried with all of his might to keep his gaze down. However, some unseen force was pulling his attention in her direction.

He looked up, and their eyes locked.

For a moment, the world stood still, the stars brightened, and the moon poured its radiant beams onto Sydney's skin. She tenderly pulled her hand up by her cheek and gave a tiny wave towards the trio. A lump formed in Jim's throat, and his lungs pulled tight. He hadn't the slightest clue what to do next. Once again, he found himself floundering in uncharted waters, with Sydney circling.

The three guys continued to walk for a couple more steps. Sydney motioned for Jim to join her, and he stopped dead in his tracks. He was paralyzed with angst.

Lance leaned close and whispered, "Atta boy, get 'er done"

Jim hesitated before complying, "Okay. I'll catch up with you guys tomorrow."

Jim smiled and continued to just stare are Sydney. He was a nervous wreck and could hardly comprehend the situation. He was still angry at her for the embarrassment she'd caused, but she was also intoxicating. He was unsure of what to do next, as Sydney slowly walked towards him.

"Hey, can I talk to you for a sec?" She said.

His hands clammed up.

"What do I say? What do I say?" He questioned himself, as she slowly moved towards him.

Blank.

Nothing.

His mind was void—simply a foreboding emptiness. However, there was no turning back now. He was right next to her and had to come up with something.

"Sure," he said, pausing a moment before continuing, "I saw you at the game. You know, in Europe, they call it futbol?"

Sydney scrunched her eyebrows, confusion written all over her face. "Um, no, I didn't know that."

"What an idiot." Jim internally punched himself. "You know, in Europe, they call it futbol? I can't believe I just said that," he continued, silently scolding himself.

His mind was racing.

"Truth be told, I'm not really much of a sports fan. But, I enjoyed the game tonight," Sydney said, breaking the silence.

Jim only mustered a quivering smile in response.

"Well, um," Sidney said. "I wanted to talk to you about something. I don't really know how to say it, so I'll just spit it out. I feel really bad about what happened in Thompson's class, and I wanted to tell you that I'm sorry."

A quiet warmth of forgiveness ran through Jim's soul.

"It's fine," he said with a hushed voice, looking off to the side. "No worries."

It became clear to Jim that that was not enough for Sidney, as she leaned to the side and forced him to make eye contact with her.

"I want to try to make it up to you. Can I take you out for pizza tonight?"

Jim felt as though there was no oxygen left on the planet. He was so startled by the question that he, once again, had no response; he just kept digging through the catacombs of his mind for something, anything to say in response.

"Oh, I can't," was all he could spit out.

Sidney once again looked confused.

"Oh, okay then. I guess I'll just get going. It was…" she began, before being cut off by a frantic Jim.

"No, no, no, I didn't mean it like that. It's just that my folks are in town tonight for the game, and they wanted to take me out for dinner."

The two remained silent for a few seconds, neither really knowing how to take the conversation any further.

"You can come with us," he finally blurted out.

"Um, I don't think so. We can go out another time."

"Okay then. How about we do pizza another night…What do

you think about that?"

"Sure, and how about I buy. Will that make it up to you?"

"Sure," Jim replied, shrugging his shoulders.

"Alright, it's a date. See you around, Superstar."

With that, she flashed a sly smile and moved to walk away.

"See yah."

"She is gorgeous," he thought to himself.

Not wanting the moment to end, he took a step toward Sydney and tried to think of something clever to say.

"When?" Was all that popped out.

Sydney turned. "When what?"

"When do you want to get pizza?"

"How about tomorrow night?" She queried. "Or are you parents still going to be around?"

"Yeah, they'll be gone."

"Tomorrow it is," she said with a small curl of her lips.

Jim turned and began to trot away. Suddenly, he realized he was again missing crucial information for their date.

He returned to Sydney. "Um, what time tomorrow?"

"Alright, let me spell it out for you," she said with a laugh. "I'll be at your dorm at six, we'll walk to Turoni's for pizza, we'll eat pizza, and then we'll walk home."

"I have a car," he nervously blurted out.

"Okay then, we'll *drive* to Turoni's for pizza, she said with a smile. "And I promise that I will have you home by ten, so you can put on your pajamas and say your prayers. How's that for a plan?"

"Great," he said, returning the smile.

The pair stood awkwardly for a few seconds before Jim took a step backwards, trying to signal that he was ready to leave for the dinner appointment with his parents.

"Don't stand me up," she joked as he walked backwards.

"Don't, worry. I'm excited," he said while slightly blushing.

After another look and a few more backward steps, Jim turned and jogged down the sidewalk, around the corner of the building. He was overpowered with exhilaration and leapt into the air, thrusting a powerful fist forward, and landing into a full on sprint. He could not wait to brag to anyone who would listen.

CHAPTER 29

OF COURSE, TOM AND Debbie knew nothing of what had been transpiring with Jim on campus. The two had been patiently waiting for their son to join them at the local burger joint for dinner. About thirty minutes late, Jim finally bounded into the restaurant out of breath. Debbie eyed her son as he hustled over to the table.

"Dad, mom, guess what?" Jim exclaimed.

They were surprised by his outburst of giddiness, especially in such a small burger joint.

"Whoa, son, you seem more excited than usual. Something happen after the game?" Tom asked.

Jim leaned forward and slapped his hands on the table, startling both his parents. "I have my first date—tomorrow night."

"Congratulations, son," Tom responded with a high five.

Debbie, on the other hand, was not quite as animated about the news. She was more than a bit apprehensive. In reality she was a little surprised that Jim had not mentioned this girl before.

"Do we know her?" She asked.

"Nope. I met her in one of my classes."

Tom cut in. "Where are you taking her?"

"She's actually taking me out."

"I'm not sure that's appropriate for a first date, son," Debbie said.

"Mooommm," Jim drew out with a bothered tone.

"C'mon Debbie, you're not that old fashioned are you?" Tom asked. "It's a new generation thing."

"I'm not old fashioned, it's just that…" Debbie trailed off and never finished her thought. She really wanted to respect her son's space—something she'd never been very good at during his high school years.

Tom finally broke the silence. "I am proud of you, son. Make sure you show her those smooth Anderson moves I taught you."

That statement rapidly brought Debbie back into the conversation. Flashbacks of their first few dates and Tom's excessive nervousness filled her mind.

"You mean like this?" She said with a sarcastic smile. "Uh, Deb… ah…Debbie, will you, um, will you go out with me?" She said with her best impression of a very nervous, college-aged Tom.

The three laughed together. For the next two hours the trio talked about the game, the first few weeks of college, and Jim's upcoming date.

CHAPTER 30

EARLY THE NEXT EVENING, Jim found himself the victim of an emotional overload. He stood anxiously at his bathroom sink. It was hard to concentrate on anything. With each hyperventilating breath, nervousness clutched a little tighter.

"Lance, what'd you do with my gel?" Jim shouted through the cracked bathroom door.

"It's probably in the drawer right where you always put it."

"Found it. You were right—in the drawer the whole time."

The only thing he could focus on for any length of time was the agonizing stress he felt for that night's date with Sydney. Frustration rushed to the surface again. "Lance, I can't find my body spray."

Lance appeared in the door frame holding a small spray can, while Jim continued to fumble frantically through the drawers.

"Dude, you're acting like you've never been on a date before."

"Thanks for the commentary," Jim responded, ripping the can from Lance's hand and nervously over-applying the potent liquid.

"Relax man," Lance tried to reassure his friend, while waving the cloud of cologne away from his face. "How could she resist your cute baby face and those buns of steel?"

With an obnoxious laugh, Lance slapped his frightened roommate on the butt and left with some final instructions. "Just go out there, have some fun, and quit acting like a loser. She's probably just a gold digger anyways, trying to cash in on your future millions. So, string her along for a ride, and get something out of it for your troubles."

Jim sternly eyed Lance in the mirror's reflection.

"You know what I mean—some serious hand-holding," Lance finished with a smile.

With that, Lance darted back to his bed to continue watching TV. Suddenly, Jim's phone lit up, and a text notification popped up on the screen. He was filled with anticipation, presuming the text was from Sydney.

"I'm outside. Where you at?" It said.

Like a freighted deer, Jim darted to his desk, grabbed his wallet, and flew out the door. Upon exiting the building, he saw Sydney rise up from a bench and walk towards him. His heart started racing, blood rushed to his head, and his vision began to blur.

"What do I do?" he asked himself. "Am I supposed to shake her hand? Give her a hug? Hold her hand? Walk her to the car?"

Luckily for Jim, these fears were short lived. Sydney reached forward and grabbed his arm so he could effortlessly escort her to his car. Jim had been so worried about what he was going to talk about, he'd spent close to an hour earlier in the day surfing the web for trending topics, and writing them down on a piece of paper that he concealed in his wallet for emergency reference. Although, once again luck was on his side, he soon learned that Sydney had the gift of gab. For the entire car ride, she carried on a conversation by herself, and it was no different at the restaurant. It seemed as if finding things to talk about that evening wasn't going to be so difficult after all.

As they sat down at their table for dinner, Sydney continued, "Well, I have one older brother and a younger sister. Want to know something else really cool?" In her typical fashion, she left little time for Jim to respond. "I will be the first in my family to graduate college."

"That's awesome," he politely responded.

"Okay, I'm doing all the talking," she said, after realizing that those were the first words Jim had uttered in about five minutes. "What about your family? Tell me about them."

"Umm, well, we're pretty boring. It's just me and my parents. I'm their only child. My mom had a hard time getting pregnant, and then couldn't have any more kids after me. She likes to say she only had room in her heart for me."

"Sounds like you have a great family."

"Yea, I have a pretty good relationship with my parents. But honestly, we are actually kind of boring."

"Having a close family does not sound boring to me," Sydney responded.

"Well, maybe boring is the wrong word. Predictable may be a better description. I spent so much of my time playing soccer. When I wasn't on the field, my Mom was always watching over my shoulder.

I couldn't really have a lot of fun getting in trouble with my friends."

"I knew it. You're a momma's boy."

"No, no—nothing like that," Jim retorted with a bit of discomfort. "When I was first born, I was really sick. In fact, the doctors didn't think I was going to make it through the first night. They wanted to hook me up to all kinds of machines, but my mom just wanted to hold me, in case I didn't make it. She wanted to be with me to the very end."

Jim paused a moment to keep his emotions in check.

"I don't think it is even possible, but I feel like I remember that night, you know? I feel like I remember my mom holding me, like I was begging her to just keep holding me. I didn't want those machines; I just wanted to be held."

He looked up at Sydney, who had compassion in her eyes. Jim quickly realized how sappy the conversation had turned.

"But I think I turned out okay, didn't I?" He said, attempting to steer the dialogue in a different direction.

"Well, I think the jury's still out on that one," she said with a smile.

A slight flush ran across Jim's face. "Yeah, maybe."

The two shared a laugh and a brief moment of personal connection.

"This is actually going pretty good," he thought to himself.

True to form, Sydney broke up the momentary silence. "So what do you want to do after college?"

"You mean, when I grow up?" He joked.

"Yeah, when you become a real boy," she said, imitating Pinocchio's voice.

"Do you really want to know?"

"Of course I do."

"Trust me, if I told you the truth, you would probably think I was out of my mind or something," he said.

"Out of your mind, huh? I know that wanting to be a professional athlete is a pipe dream for most people, but you're all over the newspapers. I bet you're going to play in the Super Bowl or Super Cup—whatever they call it."

"Yeah, I think I would like to do that, but that's just for a couple years. Sports are a fleeting endeavor, you know?"

"Yeah, but you can make a lifetime's worth of money in those few years."

Jim eyed Sydney. Lance's warning from earlier in the night flashed across his mind like the lights of Vegas.

She continued. "Well, what then? Do you want to be a sportscaster or something?"

"No, that's not it, it's just…" he paused for a few seconds to think about how he was going to proceed.

"It's kind of lame," he paused. "Alright, I want to be a high school teacher."

His face winced, and he lowered his head. But, to his pleasant surprise, Sydney didn't act in the mocking fashion he expected.

"So?" He nervously prodded.

"So? What's so weird about that?" She asked.

"I don't know. I guess I just assumed you wanted a guy that's going to be rich, like a doctor or lawyer—or maybe a professional athlete."

He let those words hang in the air for a moment.

"That's what I want, huh?" She asked. "Is that what you think of me, Jim? I'm some kind of shallow chick looking for a sugar daddy? That the only reason I am talking to you, is because you have become famous on campus?" She asked with frustration in her voice.

"No, no, no," he tried to slow down the conversation that seemed to be spiraling out of control.

"Well, I can tell you that you're dead wrong. I grew up with nothing, and nothing is what I'll always have. I don't have all these talents like you do." She leaned back in her chair as her nostrils flared with frustration.

"Thanks a lot, Lance," Jim thought to himself.

CHAPTER 31

"I'M SORRY, SYDNEY. THAT'S not what I meant. Really, I'm just a nerd, and having a girl as beautiful and wonderful as you wanting to spend time with me is making me nervous."

Sydney looked up from her irritated stare that had been pointed downwards towards the table. A sudden softness ran through her heart. She had grown up in a broken home. Her alcoholic father had relentlessly belittled her and made her feel as though she was worthless. In grade school, her mother used to refer to Sydney as, "my little ugly duckling." However, Jim had just called her beautiful; wonderful. And she could tell that he meant it.

"Sydney," he said. "I want to be honest with you. I was really hurt when you made me look like an idiot in class," he said. "But, then you came to apologize, and I knew you had a wonderful heart, and that I should immediately forgive and forget. I was so happy when I saw you on that bench outside of the locker room last night. It's just that you're one of the most amazingly beautiful creations that God has ever made, and I'm getting really nervous around you. Please know that I didn't mean that you only wanted to be my friend because I am good at soccer."

"Beautiful creation from God?" She thought to herself.

Sydney's parents had occasionally taken her to church when she was young, but she'd never believed in God. She'd never been able to find a way to reconcile how her father could profess to love Jesus on Sunday, and then drink himself into oblivion after his beloved NFL team lost. Verbal abuse had been a constant in Sydney's supposedly Christian home. She'd been very young when she'd sworn off religion. She'd seen it as something that uneducated people did to make themselves feel important; or that it was used as some mechanism for controlling others.

But, Jim did not seem to fit that mold. He was obviously a religious guy, but he was nothing like her father. He actually seemed to exemplify the principles he professed.

"Does he actually believe that I'm some kind of beautiful creation from a God?" She questioned herself again. "Does he actually believe in all that religious garbage?"

"Sydney? Sydney?" He broke her train of thought. "I'm sorry if I offended you."

She quickly realized that she had been awkwardly staring off into space—deep in her own thoughts.

"No, Jim. I believe you. And thank you for saying I'm beautiful. You're not so bad yourself, you know," she flirted, to ease the tension.

CHAPTER 32

AROUND NINE-FIFTEEN, THE EMPLOYEES at Turino's began cleaning the floors and wiping down the booths in preparation to close. The night was ending with a remarkable sunset, so the pair decided to drop Jim's car off at his dorm and walk the short distance to Sydney's apartment. Jim was spellbound by how her hair glistened in the campus lights. More than once, he caught himself staring at her beautiful smile, amazed at the ease in which she could carry on a conversation.

In his mind, it had been the perfect night. But, what he didn't realize was that Sydney was feeling the same way. Softly, she slid her arm through Jim's and gently grasped his hand. He flinched, surprised by the sudden warmth of her hand. He looked at her and was greeted by a warm smile.

"Is this what falling in love feels like?" He pondered.

Little was said between the two as they walked down the sidewalk, but volumes could have been written about the emotions Jim was feeling. The couple made their way up the small set of stairs to Sydney's front door. She quickly rotated in front of Jim, bringing him to a halt by being uncomfortably inside his personal space.

"I had a great time tonight," she sweetly said.

"Me too," he quickly replied.

A few awkward seconds passed, with only the crickets providing the spoken words. Jim was a petrified rookie and wasn't going to make the next move.

After what seemed like an eternity, Sydney had to nudge the event forward, "So?"

Standing frozen with anxiety, his lips could only spit out, "So what?"

She softly responded, "So, are you going to kiss me? Or are we going to stand here all night?"

Sheer terror debilitated Jim. Sweat was rolling down his back, and his hands clammed up. He could not utter a single word and just stood in place like a stunned deer.

"C'mon, Jim. You act like you've never kissed a girl before."

Trying his best to save face, he garbled, "Well, um, actually, I…"

She quickly realized that what she had said in jest was actually the reality. She was overflowing with excitement at the thought that she might be his first kiss. Reflexes took over, and she put both her hands to her face in surprise. "You went all the way through high school and never kissed a girl? No way. That is too cute."

She may have found it endearing, but Jim was mortified. Trying to salvage a sliver of pride, he mumbled an attempt at a rebuttal, "Well, it's just that…"

Again, he couldn't think of anything to say in the defense of his honor. He hung his head with embarrassment.

"Jim, I'm sorry. I have just…" She paused, apparently trying to come up with the right words to say. "Just never met a guy like you." Quickly catching herself again, she continued, "And, don't take that the wrong way. It's a good thing."

He continued to stare at his feet, hoping to avoid more embarrassment.

Sydney didn't let much time pass as she reached forward and gently grasped Jim's face with her soft, affectionate hands and pulled him close. His heart raced, but he was surprisingly calm. Sneaking a quick glance, he saw Sydney's lips draw near and gently touch his cheek. Sensations from the soft touch, the sweet smell of her hair, and the sound of her breath overwhelmed the young soccer star. Sydney gently released his head and he remained frozen, unable to move for a few moments. However, he was not the only one who was feeling something.

Sydney's knees slightly wobbled during their embrace. She did not anticipate feeling that strong after one simple date and a kiss on the cheek. Jim had something very peculiar about him. He didn't try to stick his tongue down her throat or grab her butt, like most of her first dates. In fact, he hadn't even tried to kiss her. For the first time in her life she could actually feel respect not lust, from a male suitor. Just like Jim, she was now in uncharted waters.

She had no time to savor the moment before her dating experience kicked in, moving her past the emotions she just felt to bring the night to a close. She tenderly turned around to face the door and slowly turned the key. Jim remained motionless, tingling from just her small peck on his cheek.

"Good night, Jim. I'll let you save your first real kiss for the one you want to share it with," she whispered with a gentle smile, before quietly passing into her apartment.

It took every ounce of focus and energy for Jim to respond back with a good night of his own. Sydney quietly closed the door and left her date standing quiet and still. Collecting himself after a few precious seconds of reflection, Jim began to meander down the sidewalk. Calm serenity rapidly morphed into euphoria. Instinctively, he began to run. With a giant leap into the air he pumped his fist and yelled, "Yes!"

He was excited to share his experience with Lance and broke into a full sprint to get back to the dorm. He blasted into his room, only to find Lance cocooned inside his blankets.

This couldn't wait.

Jim aggressively sat himself down on the edge of Lance's bed and shook him awake. "Lance! Lance! Wake up!"

"What?" Lance responded with a semi-comatose utterance.

"Hey, I'm back."

"Fantastic dude, good for you," Lance burbled sarcastically, rolling tighter into his blankets.

"It was awesome; even got a good night kiss. Well, sort of like a kiss. Close enough for me."

"Nice work. Five hundred thousand more to go and you can catch up to me," Lance said with one final roll, showing Jim he was serious about sleeping.

"I think we really hit it off. What should I do next? Should I wait for her to call me? Should I call her tonight? I need your help with my next move."

Lance remained motionless. His only response was a fake snore and some loud breathing.

"C'mon Lance. I need your advice."

No movement. Lance was out and wasn't going to hear a word. Jim's date recap would have to wait until the morning. He patted Lance on the back and said in a friendly tone, "Good night, buddy."

"Tonight was incredible." Jim smiled to himself.

CHAPTER 33

JIM'S FEELINGS SPILLED OVER into the next day. At the afternoon practice, his newfound confidence with the ladies manifested itself into obnoxious and immature behavior. His teammates were perplexed by the scene that was playing out before them. They had become accustomed to practices filled with focus and discipline; Jim leading the way. On that day, however, this was hardly the case. He was bouncing around the field with juvenility. Lance was standing next to Bryant while they waited in line for a practice drill.

"Did you slip something in his food this morning?" Bryant leaned over and asked Lance.

"Nope, it's a girl."

"Jim? A girl? I'll believe it when I see it."

At that very moment, Jim blasted a shot past the goalie. The ball hissed with speed as it traveled through the air.

"Yes!" He yelled, while pumping his fist in the air.

"Dude, chill! You're freaking everyone out," Bryant yelled across the field.

Seemingly undeterred, Jim ran by Bryant with a huge grin on his face. "Who's the man now?" He barked while racing off for another shot.

Bryant looked over, at Lance and said, "You need to calm that guy down, before be explodes."

Lance shrugged in reply. He had no intention of slowing Jim down. He was actually quite pleased to see him screwing around. Lance loved soccer, but never had had the intensity that Jim possessed. Plus, he felt it was quite refreshing to have a relaxing practice for once.

CHAPTER 34

ON THE OTHER SIDE of campus, Sydney had decided once again to take a different route home from class. She was determined to see Jim, and to show off the outfit she had purchased specifically for this kind of occasion. As she walked closer to the field, one by one, the players began to take notice. Her muscular, tanned legs seemed to stretch for miles, before ending at a pair of authoritative black heels. She'd donned a short, frilly skirt and a tight red top—just form-fitting enough to keep the players looking for more.

After slowly arriving at the sidelines, she positioned herself next to the bleachers. With a bend of her knee and a purposeful kink in her spine, she waved in Jim's direction. He didn't seem to notice her, and she was determined to make her presence felt so she stretched just a little bit higher on her toes.

"Hey Superstar," she called out with an air of sensuality.

Jim finally looked toward the direction of the call. He suddenly stopped as their eyes connected, allowing the ball at his feet to roll aimlessly to a defensive player.

CHAPTER 35

"WOW!" JIM THOUGHT TO himself.

His heart raced above its already elevated, scrimmage-induced rate, and his chest tightened with excitement, making it even harder to breath. Testosterone was thrashing through his veins. Never in his life had he seen a girl look so beautiful, especially not one who was yelling for his attention.

"Hey, Sydney, how's it going?" He yelled.

"Great! Just came to see your practice."

Coach Peterson had been watching the entire scene play out, and he was not happy. The last thing he needed for his star player was more distraction.

"Jim, get your head in the game," he roared.

Startled by the command, Jim snapped back to reality.

"Oops. Sorry, coach."

Jim gave Sydney one last wave. She put her hand to her ear, extended her thumb and pinkie in the shape of a phone, and mouthed, "Call me."

Bryant and Lance stayed fixated on Sydney's long, seductive legs as she walked away.

"I'm afraid for him," Bryant said to Lance.

"Yeah—join the club."

Jim ran by his stunned teammates. "Who's got mojo now, boys?"

"Mojo? Seriously dude—I'm very afraid," Lance continued to Bryant. "He's like a little white lamb walking right into the slaughterhouse."

CHAPTER 36

JUST A FEW WEEKS passed, and the odds of Jim and Sydney falling together down the rabbit hole of love should have been slim at best. Yet, there they were at each other's side, day and night. Even when they were physically separated, their blossoming romance kept them mentally connected. This bond was no more evident than during halftime at the next home game. All Jim could think of was Sydney.

"Mike," Jim whispered inside the locker room at halftime, grabbing the athletic trainer's arm.

"Yeah, Jim?"

"You got a pencil, or a pen and paper?"

"I think so. Let me check my bag."

"Great," Jim replied with an unusual amount of excitement.

Mike grabbed his equipment bag, fished around for a moment, and then handed a pen and small scrap of paper to Jim.

"Thanks man," Jim responded, putting the paper against the side of the locker to write. Mike was looking curiously over Jim's shoulder to see what was going on. Sensing his inquisitive stare, Jim moved his body closer to the locker to shield what he was writing. After a few quick scratches of the pen, he folded the paper to the size of a quarter and put it inside the top of his sock.

"Thanks, Mike," he stated, tossing back the pen.

"No problem," Mike replied.

After a quick salute, Jim ran out of the locker room to join his teammates for the second half. The sun had fully retired on the horizon, and flood lights now illuminated the field. Everyone loved to play under the lights. The grass felt different under the hue of the luminescent bulbs, seeming to change in color to a darker blue-green.

Upon entering the field, Jim immediately looked over in the direction where Sydney had been sitting. She was nowhere to be seen. A little concerned, he slowed down to a walk, trying to make it easier to locate the girl of his dreams. Within a few seconds, he had spotted her returning from the snack bar. The lights lit up around her as if she was an angel floating down the side of the field. He was hypnotized by the beauty of her countenance.

Typically, Jim played in the center of the field as a striker. In the second half of that night's game, however, he continually favored the right side. He was so out of position at times that he confused his own teammates, and they were making uncharacteristic mistakes. These adjustments were intentional, though—Jim had a plan.

He eventually received a pass close to the sideline; as an opposing player moved in close to defend. Oddly, Jim seemed to intentionally kick the ball off the leg of the defender and out of bounds, toward where Sydney was sitting. Evansville was awarded the throw-in. His teammates gave him looks of confusion, once again, as he quickly waved off his right midfielder, who typically took most of the throw-ins on that side of the field. Jim ran to pick up the ball, which had conveniently come to rest near the bleachers, less than a meter from Sydney's feet. Pulling the little note of out his sock, he made an attempt to discretely drop it in her lap. He was embarrassed that everyone may have seen what he did, so he quickly threw the ball back into play and prayed that no one noticed.

Sydney was visibly startled by the event, as she fumbled around to retrieve the small piece of paper. Out of the corner of his eye, Jim saw Sydney slowly unfold the note while the curious eyes of those around her peered in. Obviously annoyed, she leaned forward so no one could see the contents of what Jim had just dropped in her lap.

Jim replayed what he had written in his mind as he watched Sydney read the note. "You're the most amazing women I have ever met! I can't stop thinking about you! What a blessing you are to me!"

It was a simple note, possibly immature and a bit cheesy. But for Jim, it took a lot of courage. Outward shows of affection were not something he had done much of in his young life.

Even from fifteen yards away, Jim could see that Sydney was fighting back tears. Suddenly, she shot up out of her seat and bolted off the field. She was running down the sideline, only stopping for a short moment to take off her heals so she could run faster.

"Oh no; that was too much. I've blown it," he thought with panic.

The rest of the game became a blur. All Jim could think about was the ref blowing the whistle to end the match. Finally, the signal came. The final score: Home—two; Visitors—one. Not one for the highlight reel, but it was nonetheless a win for Evansville. After the traditional congratulatory handshakes, Jim trudged back to the bench to grab his equipment bag, before heading to the locker room.

CHAPTER 37

J IM WAS CONFUSED AND upset. Only negative thoughts raced through his mind; about what he had written on the note, and his uncanny ability to let the most beautiful woman he had ever encountered slip through his fingers. Their relationship had been developing at an incredible rate, but he'd never imagined that tossing her a simple, heartfelt message would bring the whole thing tumbling down. Memories of a teenage life filled with failed attempts at dating bombarded his consciousness. Evidently, this episode with Sydney was just another disappointment to add to the list. But this time the hurt was more profound. Jim was numb, lost to the point where all the noises around him were nothing more than a fog of confusion.

He quietly packed up his gear and headed out the locker room door to the parking lot. Too his surprise he saw Sydney leaning against one of the trees that ran in parallel with the sidewalk. He'd figured she would have been long gone by then. All he could assume was that her presence signaled that the end was near. He quickened his pace in her direction, figuring that closing the gap would help rip the bandage off just a little faster. Sydney pushed herself up from her lean and moved in his direction.

As the two closed within earshot, Jim began, "Sydney, I'm so sorry. I didn't mean to…"

He was suddenly cut off as she rushed towards him.

"Is she going to hit me?" He quickly asked himself, slowing to a defensive stance.

Sydney was undeterred by anything Jim was doing and continued her relentless approach. With a swift, yet beautiful movement, she reached forward, placed both her hands around the back of his neck, and passionately kissed him. The heat from her lips lit up Jim's body like a match to gasoline. Something about the kiss felt so right. Slowly, he wrapped his arms around her waist and returned the kiss by tilting his head into a natural position. The power of their bond fired through his soul. In that instant, Jim knew that he had nothing to worry about.

After a few magical seconds, Sydney slowly pulled her head away, her bottom lip momentarily sticking to his—adhering the passion for just a second longer. She looked deeply into his eyes as he looked into hers, a connection burning deep into their hearts, infinitely more profound than any physical attraction.

"How was that for your first real kiss?" She said.

Jim could only smile in response.

Lance interrupted the fairytale moment. "Hey, you two. Think you can keep your clothes on long enough to come with us for pizza and a few drinks?"

Neither of them responded to Lance. They were both still lost in the moment.

Lance continued, "You know, I would score more goals, if I wasn't so distracted during the game by the love fest going on between you two."

Jim couldn't help himself and responded, "Well, maybe if you wouldn't sail the ball thirty feet over the top of the net every time I pass it to you, you'd have more than Sydney and me to focus on."

Lance laughed and looked at Sydney. "What you'd do to this guy?"

"Nothing; he's just that good," she responded while stealing another kiss from Jim.

"You know what? Coach may have to ban you from the rest of the games," Lance said while playfully pointing at Sydney. "We're at the top of the division right now—a place Evansville has never found itself, for your information. We need this guy!"

CHAPTER 38

THE MOOD WAS NOT as jovial at the Anderson home. Debbie sat impatiently on the couch reading a book. Every couple of minutes, she couldn't help but shoot an anxious look towards the phone sitting on the end table. Her mind was half on the book and half on trying to understand why Jim hadn't called to recap the game. After another agonizing thirty minutes, Debbie finally decided to give into the truth—Jim had forgotten to call. Let down with growing feelings of self-pity, she quietly stared at the phone with a couple of final, lingering breaths.

A deep voice from the top of the stairs startled her from her thoughts. "You coming to bed?"

"Yeah, be right up," she responded with disappointment.

Jim would not being calling that night.

CHAPTER 39

AFTER DINNER, THE COUPLE made their usual walk back to Sydney's apartment. They stood outside her front door, holding each other close. The night was storybook perfect; the sky above them was a crisp black with an endless smattering of angelic points filling the void. The air was filled with a calm serenity, and the perfume of dew accented the scene. Jim's confidence around Sydney had finally grown to match his swagger on the field. This supply of courage helped him initiate a long good night kiss.

"You want to come in?" Sydney asked after the kiss. "My roommates are gone for the weekend."

"No, I better get going."

"Jim," she softly emphasized her point. "We have the place to ourselves."

Her intentions became instantly apparent to Jim. He tried to skirt the issue, to maintain the perfect night. The last thing he wanted was to test his moral convictions about pre-marital sex.

"No, really, I can't. I think I should get…"

"It's okay Jim," she softly reassured. "I'll teach you everything you need to know. I can promise you, it will be the most amazing night of your life."

The peace he had previously experienced quickly vanished and his heart leapt, the pull of testosterone screaming through his body. The lust-filled animal was tearing him inside, attempting to rise to the surface. He tried another, last ditch effort to quell the beast. "I'm sorry, Syd—you just don't understand. I can't. I made a promise."

Her face filled with visible frustration and confusion. She snapped back, "A promise about what?"

Jim was besieged with embarrassment. He certainly didn't want to end the date like this. He released his grip around her waist and tried to explain. "I made a promise to God, that I won't do that stuff until I'm married. I want to save it for that special person."

Sydney's demeanor immediately turned cold. "So, what are you're saying, Jim? I mean, I know we're not married. But are you saying that I am not that special person?"

"No, that's not it. You just don't understand."

"You don't think I understand?" She loudly barked. "Am I stupid, too?"

"No, no, no, I like you so much. You're just…"

Sydney immediately cut him off. Surprised and hurt, she continued, "I'm just what, Jim? I'm not good enough for your church or God or whatever? You're always talking about it. So, am I just some kind of harlot, or some immoral sinner or something? Is that it Jim?"

"Sydney, no. Please don't do this," he pleaded. "You're just…"

She, once again, cut him off. This time, she pushed his lingering hands away from her hips. "You know, Jim, you're right. I don't understand anything about you. I don't understand your cult. I don't understand your stupid promise. I don't..."

"Sydney, it's not like that," Jim tried to amend the situation once more.

"Look, this was never going to work anyway. You knew it, I knew it," Sydney said with tears filling up in her eyes. "We're just too different."

Before Jim could get in another word, Sydney turned and ran into her apartment. With the slam of the door, he was left in the dark of the night.

Alone.

Confused.

Rejected.

"What just happen?" He replayed the scene.

He tried to regain his composure. Every synapse of his mind was screaming to knock on the door and explain what he meant with his promise. But the once lustful beast had instantly morphed into despair and was dragging him down into a dark place. Jim turned away and faded into the night.

Dejected.

Broken.

"Maybe I really am a self-righteous jerk," he thought to himself, wallowing in abandon while wandering aimlessly through campus. He eventually found himself staring blankly at the night sky while sitting on a park bench. His thoughts were full of loneliness and desolation. He had no tears; the hopelessness was too painful for any trite waterworks.

CHAPTER 40

ARLY THE NEXT MORNING, Jim was startled back to life by the ring of his cell. He quickly recognized the call was from his mother—she had her own ringtone. Barely conscious and still devastated from the events of the previous evening, he slid his thumb across the screen.

"Yeah?" He coarsely answered.

"Jim?" She questioned with concern in her tone.

"Mom, it's six in the morning."

"What happened last night, son?"

His mind immediately sprung to life.

"How does she know what happened?" He questioned himself.

"What do you mean last night?" He asked, probing to see how much his mother already knew about the doorstep episode.

"What do I mean? I waited up all night to hear how your game went, but you never called."

He breathed a sigh of relief. His mother did not know about

the epic failure with Sydney. However, her inadvertent reminder of that episode only a couple of hours before reawakened the depressive creature inside Jim.

"C'mon mom; I'm not a little kid anymore," he raised his voice, waking Lance. "I went out with Sydney after the game. Is that okay with you, or do I need to ask you if I can do that?"

"Son, please don't talk like that. What's going on?"

Jim heard the mattress squeak and looked to see that he had woken up Lance.

"Look mom; I'm sick of you trying to run my life. Can I go back to sleep now?"

His rude retort must have been shocking enough for Lance, the antithesis of a morning person, because he sat up in his bed and stared directly at Jim with disbelief. On the other end of the line, the sounds of a sniffle and a cracked voice let Jim know that tears were flowing. The stinging words from her son must have come as a total surprise. Obviously, Debbie hadn't been prepared for this barrage of anger when she made the call. Not knowing how to respond, she surrendered with a heartrending, "Fine son, if that's how you want to talk to me."

"Great, now you're going to pull that woe-is-me crap. Whatever." Jim abruptly hung up the phone and looked at his inquisitive roommate.

"Dude, what's going on?" Lance asked.

"Nothing. I don't want to talk it," Jim shot back while turning his back to his friend.

"You know, if I had a mom like yours, I wouldn't talk to her like that," Lance said.

Jim said nothing in return and remained motionless in bed. He knew the way he had just talked to him mom was completely out of line. However, the despair of his soul seemed to completely cloud his ability to put other's above himself.

CHAPTER 41

DEBBIE WAS STUNNED BY Jim's behavior, and her tears quickly stopped as she shifted to a defensive posture. She looked over at Tom, who was innocently reading the news on his phone at the kitchen table, and commanded, "That's it. We're driving to every one of Jim's games."

"What?" Tom asked with his eyebrows raised in confusion.

"Every one! I'm going to all his games."

"What about my annual work banquet? Isn't there a game on that night?"

"Who cares? You can go to the dumb banquet, but I'm driving to see Jim."

Before Tom could react, Debbie stormed out the kitchen.

CHAPTER 42

THE NEXT DAY, SYDNEY decided to call Lance, because Jim wouldn't answer his phone.

"Talk to me," Lance answered the way he always did.

"Lance, is Jim there? He's not answering my calls, and I need to talk to him."

"I think he's outside kicking a ball around."

"Did he tell you anything about last night?" She hesitantly asked.

"Not much, but you must have really torched him, because he yelled at his mom on the phone at like six in the morning. It was really weird."

Sydney hesitated for a moment before posing another timid question. "Do you think he'll talk to me?"

"I hope so. You better get over here before he hurts himself. I'm looking at him out my window right now. He's talking to himself and blasting soccer balls against the wall of the dorm next to us."

A slight smile crossed her face, as the prospect of being able to talk to Jim again gave her some hope.

"Thanks," she said, hanging up the phone.

After she had closed the door on Jim the night before, she snuck over to the window and watched him fad away into the night. Tears had flowed freely down her cheeks, accompanied by gut-wrenching sobs. Jim had rejected her advance, and it had hurt. All she could surmise was the realization that maybe her mom had been right– Sydney was just a sinful, ugly duckling. She had opened herself up to Jim, and his rejection was humiliating. However, after a long night of self-reflection, she had made peace. And reconciling with Jim was more important than trying to cover up her puffy, mascara-stained face.

She quickly pulled her hair into a ponytail and rushed out the door. When Jim came into view, she slowed her pace. Lance was right. Jim was visibly upset and was punishing a soccer ball against a wall with frenzied kicks. She nervously approached from behind.

"Jim, will you talk to me?" Sydney politely asked, her voice shaking with nervousness.

"Nope," he responded as immature as is voice would allow.

"Look—I don't know what happened last night."

The slam of another ball against the bricks let off a thundering boom, echoing through the dorm complex. Sydney flinched with the sound, but carried on undeterred.

"It's just," she paused to find the words. "I've never met anyone like you before."

"You mean a self-righteous mamma's boy? You mean some freaky cult-worshipper?" He popped off, while turning his back and running off to retrieve the ball.

She yelled in his direction, "Jim, I'm really trying to apologize here. It's different with you. I don't know what I can say to let you know that I'm serious. Please, I feel horrible."

Watching him run to get the ball, Sydney was becoming more and more dejected with each passing second. She didn't know how to continue and was filled with shame. She slowly turned her back and began to walk home.

"No," Jim thought to himself. "What am I doing? I can't do this. I know better than this."

He dove deep into his spirituality, hoping to find something to help him climb out of his bitterness. He said a silent prayer. A rapid, silent reflection burned the Christ-like feeling of unconditional love into his heart. The banner of pride quickly fell as he remembered the teachings of his youth. He immediately dropped the ball and sprinted toward Sydney. With a tight grasp of her arm, he passionately spun her around to face him.

"Sydney, look—I don't know what happened last night, either. I don't know why I said the things I said."

"I know, Jim, I just…"

He politely cut her off. "Sydney, I know. We are two very different people, with two different backgrounds, but there's something special between us. I don't know what it is, but I can feel it, and I know you feel it too. I know you do, or else you wouldn't be here right now."

Tears began to well up in her eyes.

"I just think we need to spend some more time getting to know each other, before we get any more serious. Is that okay with you?"

"Yes, and I'm sorry that I called you a cult freak. All I ever learned about Mormons is that they have fifty wives and live in the mountains in Utah. Maybe you can teach me a little bit more about your religion."

"I would love to, but for now," he paused before reaching forward for a deep hug. "I want you to know that I'm deeply sorry, too. You're incredibly special to me, and I want you to know that."

Sydney's entire life had been a rollercoaster of emotions, littered with undeserved abuse and turmoil. But now there was a man who wanted nothing more than to be the opposite of that for her. She hadn't seen it at first. Jim was confusing. He was peculiar. It had taken time for her to realize that his true commitments were engrained into who he was. She now understood that he was looking for something deeper—more lasting—not merely the thrill of a few fleeting moments of physical pleasure.

CHAPTER 43

SYDNEY AND JIM QUICKLY put the incident behind them and continued to deepen their relationship. Beliefs, hopes, dreams, and all the things that made them who they were became frequent topics of discussion. Jim also spent time trying to patch up his relationship with his mother. He had apologized and decided to be more sensitive to her feelings. Things were looking up for Jim. In fact, things had improved so much that he actually had the guts to schedule a dinner with his mother, so that she could meet Sydney in person.

It was Friday night, just before the start of a game. Jim was tying up his cleats, when Bryant sat down on the bench beside to him and said, "You're in a good mood tonight. Did you finally give in and drink a beer?"

"Nope; just happy to be alive," Jim said while fist bumping Bryant. "Plus, my mom is going to meet Sydney tonight."

"Really? What's she going to think when Sydney comes strutting to dinner in a mini skirt?"

"I don't know; hadn't thought about that yet. I guess, I'll just go with the flow."

"Good for you. I knew you'd pick up some of my skills sooner or later," Bryant said while getting up from the bench and playfully pushing Jim's head.

Out on the field, it only took Jim a few minutes into warm-ups to spot his mom entering through the chain link fence.

"Coach, can you give me a sec?" He asked, pointing to the entrance.

"Hustle up," Coach Peterson responded with an impatient growl.

Jim sprinted to the sideline and gave his mom a welcome hug.

"Come sit over here by Sydney, mom," he said, while pointing to his new love. "Mom, this is Sydney."

Sydney quickly rose to her feet to greet Jim's mom. She had been mentally preparing for this moment all day. Although, all the preparation in the world could not have calmed her nerves. Debbie, too, was surprised to be meeting her son's girlfriend, so soon after arriving to the game. She'd figured they would most likely meet up as a group after the game, on the way to dinner. Unfortunately, that was no longer an option. Debbie would have to sit for the entire game beside Jim's first real girlfriend.

"Nice to meet you, Sydney. Jim has told me a lot about you. In fact, he never seems to stop talking about you."

"All good things, I hope." Sydney smiled and squeezed Jim's hand—sending the signal that she was hoping for confirmation that she was saying the right things.

Jim turned and winked at Sydney with agreement before cutting in, "Got to get back to warm-ups. You ladies have fun getting to know each other. We'll all get together after the game. This is awesome!"

As Jim turned to run back to the field, Debbie yelled her phrase of encouragement she used to start every match, "Game on, Jim!"

Sydney watched and wanted to give some encouragement of her own, "give-um hell!"

Debbie was a little surprised by Sydney's language, but was resolute to do her best to support Jim's dating decisions. She had been a very caring person and loving mother. However, this was a first for her. With all of those soccer practices and games growing up, Jim had rarely had time for a personal life. Debbie had seldom entertained Jim's friends at the house, and having girls visit had been about as rare as having an endangered panther sitting in a tree in their backyard. She was having to learn on the fly, and she felt very much like a ship without a compass. She had dedicated so much of her life to her family, that, like Jim, she was not very good at developing relationships or meeting people for the first time.

Within the first few minutes that night, it became obvious to every spectator around the field that Jim was going to dominate play. His first goal came quickly—blasting a shot from twenty yards out. The crowd went wild, and Jim joined his team for the celebration. Something was different that night. Muscle memory kicked in, and, just like his childhood years, he raised his hand above his head and gave the hand salute to his mom—this time, with his fingers curved. Debbie's heart swelled with pride, as she realized how long it had been since she'd seen that sign on the field. She raised her hand in return.

Sydney, intrigued, watched the interaction between the mother and son. The finger gun was something Sydney had seen after virtually every score, but returning the sign was never something that had occurred to her. She'd always assumed Jim was acting like some kind of cowboy, or doing the Stormin' Mormon thing. After watching Debbie and Jim's interaction, she instantly understood that the sign had some sort of meaning, and she wanted to be a part of it. She also raised her hand into the air, mimicking the sign and cheering loudly for her boyfriend.

Jim pointed to where the two women were sitting, grinning from ear–to-ear. He was totally oblivious to the situation that was about to unfold on the sideline. Debbie looked over at Sydney and felt the thud of jealousy.

"Who does she think she is?" She fumed inside.

Sydney had just, unknowingly, trampled on sacred ground, and Debbie felt somewhat betrayed. The rest of the soccer game became a frazzled blur for the proud mother. Everything Jim did was inconsequential. She couldn't get Sydney off her mind. The resentment building inside of Debbie spread like a cancerous tumor each time she glanced in Sydney's direction. Removing herself from the situation seemed to be the only option. She stood up and turned to Sydney.

"I'm going to get a hotdog."

Sydney eagerly replied, trying to make a good impression, "Okay; want me to come with you?"

"No. You stay and watch the game. I will be really quick. How about I bring you back something?"

"Great," Sydney smiled. "Could you get me a soda? Here, let me give you some money."

"No, it's my treat."

"Okay. Thanks, Mrs. Anderson."

CHAPTER 44

AFTER FIFTEEN MINUTES, DEBBIE hadn't returned, and Sydney became worried that maybe she had gotten lost; or that maybe she had offended Debbie somehow. She began to think that it might be time for her to get up and track Debbie down herself. However, Debbie shortly appeared with a hotdog and two drinks in hand.

Throughout the remainder of the game, apprehension morphed to tension between the two women. Sydney tried to engage in conversation several times, but Debbie kept her answers short and cold. Both were eager for time to expire and the game to come to an end. When the final whistle blew, Jim grabbed his equipment bag and ran to the showers after an easy win. He dressed as quickly as possible, excited to spend the rest of the evening with the two most important women in his life.

Sydney was the first to greet Jim with an enthusiastic hug as he exited the locker room.

"You were amazing tonight," she said before turning to Debbie.

"It must have been your presence, Mrs. Anderson."

A half-hearted smile was all Debbie could muster. "Nice game, son. I'm proud of you."

"Thanks Mom; it was so great that you could make it. Are we still okay for everybody to do dinner?" He enthusiastically asked the group.

At that point, he was unaware of the tension that had developed between the two women. Everyone nodded with agreement.

"Outstanding," he exclaimed while slapping his hands together. "My car is right over here."

He tenderly wrapped his arm around Sydney's waist and led the group to his car. It was lonely for Debbie to walk behind her son and his girlfriend. With a perfect, gentlemanly gesture, Jim opened the front passenger door, and Sydney was about to get in before she paused. "I'm sorry, Mrs. Anderson. Do you want to sit in the front seat?"

"No, no, you sit in the front," Debbie said with a hint of sadness in her voice.

Sydney withdrew, slid into the seat, and put on her seatbelt. Jim finally sensed the tension but didn't have enough grasp on the details to attempt any kind of mediation. All he could do was cautiously start the car and begin the short drive to the restaurant.

At dinner, Jim and Sydney sat on one side of the table, Debbie on the other. To his dismay, the tension never seemed to dissipate during the dinner.

"How can Jim's mom be so insecure?" Sydney thought to herself.

Reaching across the table, she grabbed Jim's arm and put it around her shoulder, snuggling in for an affectionate kiss on the cheek.

"You have such an adorable son," she said to Debbie with a large smile.

A slight blush came over Jim's face. Debbie did her best to ignore the feelings of loss she was having and gave a small, "thank you," in return.

When the dinner finally came to an end, the group returned to Jim's car. Once inside, Sydney turned around, and attempted to make one last effort to connect with Jim's mom. "That was really fun. Thanks for dinner and everything, Mrs. Anderson. But, mostly, thanks for raising such an amazing son."

"You're welcome," was all Debbie said in return.

The quick drive back to campus was silent, except for the radio. As Jim pulled the car in front of the apartment, Sydney turned around to speak to Debbie.

"It was great to finally meet Jim's Mom." She then looked at Jim, pulled his chin in her direction and planted a long, good night kiss on his lips. "See you tomorrow, Jim."

"See you," he blissfully replied, quickly looking into the rear view mirror to gauge his mother's reaction.

"Mom, why don't you get in the front seat?" He requested.

"I'm okay. I'm fine back here."

"C'mon, Mom," he lovingly pleaded. "Get in the front, so we can talk on the way back to your car."

She reluctantly opened the back door and moved into the front.

"So, what do you think?" He asked.

"I think you played great tonight."

"No, mom; that's not what I meant. What do you think about Sydney?"

"Well, she's definitely not shy."

"She's great. You'll understand when you get to know her better. I really like her."

"Yeah, I can tell. I guess you have the freedom to choose, right?" She said.

Jim sensed the continued uneasiness and wanted to rid his car of the feeling. He tried to divert the conversation. "Thanks for driving up. You have no idea how much it means to me. Are you sure you don't want to find a hotel and spend the night? It's pretty late."

"No, I need to get back to your father. I'll be fine."

"Okay, just call me when you get home, so I know you're safe," Jim requested as they pulled up to the parking lot.

Debbie slowly opened the front passenger door and got out of the vehicle. After only one step from the side of the vehicle, she turned around, "Jim, I, I'm..." she hesitated, to carefully craft her response. "I'm concerned about you."

"Concerned about what? I'm doing great here. Classes are going well, and the team is undefeated. I thought being away from home was going to be really tough, but I'm starting to get used to it."

"It's not that. I'm just not so sure about the choice of your first steady girlfriend."

"Mom, come on. She's great. I really want you to like her," he pleaded.

"Son, you're just eighteen."

"So?" He interrupted.

"You're way too young to get into this serious of a relationship. And, what about your church mission?"

"I'm still planning on going on a mission after this season. There's no reason I can't have a girlfriend before I leave. Plenty of guys do it. Plus, then I'll have someone to write me, while I'm gone for two years."

"Son, I don't think that girl is the type of person that cares about a selfless, caring relationship. I mean, what are you going to do when she expects more than a kiss? I don't think she has the same moral values as you."

"Get out of your bubble, mom—and her name is Sydney," he sternly rebuked. "She likes me for who I am—standards and all. We had a problem at first, but since I explained it to her, we've been fine. I'd be nice if you'd trust me like she does and let me explain it to you."

"I am sorry for how that came out, and I didn't mean to speak about Sydney like that and upset you, son. I just don't want to see you get hurt."

"I know, mom. I feel something special when I am around her. Will you please put away your judgment for just a little bit and try to get to know her? The first time I met Sydney, I did the same thing you're doing. But, I learned quickly that I was making a big mistake."

"You're an adult now, and I can't tell you what to do. I just don't think she's right for you, and I think you'll get your heart broken and bloodied in this relationship. Trust me," she said while turning around and opening the door to her car.

She slumped into the driver's seat of her own car and closed the door before rolling down the window for the last word, "Just be careful, son."

"Yah, thanks for coming mom," he muttered to himself with frustration. "It was great to see you, too."

Debbie slowly moved her car into reverse and drove about a quarter mile down the road before she had to pull over. The emotions were too much. She wept while laying her forehead against the steering wheel. It was becoming almost unbearable for her to see her son, someone who she had cared for so deeply, fade off into his own adult life. She wanted Little J back but knew that time's relenting march forward was nothing she could control.

CHAPTER 45

THE NEXT DAY, THE rise of the sun broke with beautiful colors and warmed the plains of the Midwest. However, the chill inside the Anderson home remained as cold as the dead of night. Inside the laundry room, Debbie was visibly distracted while sorting the colors from the whites. Tom emerged in the doorway, clad in pajama bottoms and a wrinkled oversized t-shirt. He was still in a half-slumber and confused as to why she was up so early.

Tom asked, "I didn't hear you get up. Is everything okay?"

She continued sorting the clothes, making no attempt at eye contact. "Couldn't sleep. I didn't want to wake you."

"Are you sure everything is okay? In twenty years of marriage, I don't think I have ever seen you do laundry on a Saturday."

"Please, Tom, everything is fine."

"Did something happen with Jim last night?" He had to pose the question.

"Absolutely not," she fibbed. "He played great."

"That's not really what I meant. I mean, is this about Jim and

Sydney?" Tom knew he was correct, but he also knew that he had to lead gently with a few intro questions, before they could peacefully get there. "So, what do you think of her?"

"Do you think I need to keep paying more for this expensive soap?" Debbie asked, while staring at a pair of pants. "We don't have stains like Jim used to get. There are less expensive soaps that could save us some money."

"No, keep buying the good stuff," he lovingly replied, moving over to rub her shoulders.

She broke the silence and brought the short shoulder rub to a halt. "I'm going to quit my job."

"Quit? Why?"

A small tear welled up in her eye and began to roll down her cheek. She hunched forward and dropped the pair of pants she had been folding on the table. Tom could instantly sense the pain that his beloved wife was feeling inside. He realized that this was not a time for additional questioning. His wife needed comfort, and his love was so deep that, without question, he would provide that comfort for her. Tenderly, he turned Debbie around and pulled her close.

"It will be okay, honey," he whispered grasping her tight.

Debbie was wrapped up in pain and tried to push away. However, his strong, devoted arms would not let her escape from his embrace. After a couple seconds, she broke down and sobbed on his shoulder.

"It will be okay," he softly repeated.

No further words were required. The cure was simple. She needed him, a dedicated man, selflessly devoted to her happiness. He would hold her until the end of time, if that's what it took.

CHAPTER 46

LATER THAT DAY, THE youngest of the Anderson family was having a much different conversation with the woman with whom he was quickly falling in love. The weather was perfect for a picnic. Jim and Sydney decided to pack a couple of snacks and head to the park on the south side of campus. They walked around for a moment before finding a great spot beneath a large shade tree. Jim pulled a couple of sandwiches, a bag of chips, and a pair of water bottles from his backpack.

"So how did you get so good at soccer?" Sydney asked as he snacked on a handful of chips.

"I don't know," he mumbled, with a few pieces flying from his mouth. "Really, I think it's mostly just a blessing from God."

"So hard work and practice had nothing to do with it?" She asked.

"Well, of course. But honestly, I have always been good at soccer. It truly has just been a gift from above."

"Well, I'm sure that God probably had less to do with it than you think."

"You really believe that?"

"Yeah, I'm not too sure how I feel about the whole Jesus thing…"

Today was the first time Jim had heard Sydney verbally communicate reservations about the existence of God. The two had had multiple conversations about religion, but Sydney always seemed to skirt the issue, by just agreeing with everything Jim said. She had told him about her Christian upbringing, although it was now becoming clearer that she possessed very little personal faith.

"Well, answer me this, Jim. There is so much ugliness and bad news everywhere. How would a god who supposedly loves us let all of that happen?"

"I don't believe that's God," Jim confidently stated. "I mean, God created this world for us. He gives us what we need and then allows us the freedom to make decisions about what we do. For me, I've found that I am most happy when I try to follow God. People are the ones that choose to do evil things. What you and I do with our ability to make choices is up to us."

"Whoa, careful Jim. You're starting to sound like a pastor. Do you have some kind of secret life as a preacher man?" She asked with a playful poke to his side.

He laughed before continuing. "No, nothing like that. I'm just telling you what I believe. I know that I can't definitively prove to you that God exists, but I also can't definitively prove to you that He doesn't. It's a matter of faith in both instances. I mean, if you need some evidence, look at all the beautiful stuff around—the sun, trees, the stars, and your eyes. There had to be a God that made all that."

"My eyes?" She asked while, batting her lashes in a seductive manner.

"Among other things," he responded, while raising his eyebrows a couple of times.

"Jim, are you saying what I think you're saying?

"No, no, nothing like that," Jim said while flushing red.

"Relax, preacher boy; I was just kidding. Plus, you've got that promise to keep. I mean... You've got the freedom to choose to keep that promise."

Jim smiled.

"See, I was listening," Sydney said.

After the laughter died down, Sydney was ready to move on to a more serious topic. "I don't think your mom likes me at all."

"What are you talking about? Of course she likes you."

"Seriously, I can tell. I'm good at this kind of thing, you know. She was really cold around me during the game and at dinner."

He paused for a moment to recollect. "I bet she was just surprised that you gave me the sign last night."

"What are you talking about? I didn't have a sign. I've never brought a sign to any of the games."

Jim said while holding up his hand, "No, not like a poster. I mean this."

He made the special sign.

"I thought that's your victory gun thing, isn't it?"

Jim smiled and sat up for a further explanation. "Okay, look. It's not really a gun. If you curve your thumb and finger a little it's actually half a heart. I have been doing this secret hand signal with my mom since I was a little kid. I made it up, because I was embarrassed to tell her that I loved her in public."

Sydney was stunned at this revelation. Her facial expression strained with distress.

"You know, my Mom must have seen you give me the sign, and it probably just shocked her a bit. It's always just been a thing just between me and her."

"Jim! I had no idea that was something special between you and your mom. Why didn't you tell me about it?"

"It's fine. She'll get over it," he assured her.

"I doubt it. She probably hates my guts—probably thinks I'm trying to cut in on her territory and steal you away from your family or something."

"Don't worry. I'm sure it's no big deal."

"I do worry, Jim. At least I had a shot at your parents liking me. I hardly ever see mine, and they were barely around when I was growing up."

"I'm sure that's not true," he said in defense of her parents.

"No, it's true. When I was cheerleading in high school, I would always hope they would show up to see me, but it rarely happened. Most of the time I would just look around and see all the other girls hugging their parents and taking pictures. It was horrible."

Jim's heart hurt for Sydney. He had a hard time even imaging his parents not attending all his activities. His parents had been so involved in his life, that it was almost impossible to envision anything different.

Sydney paused a moment before continuing. "Hey, let's stop talking about my lame childhood, it's killing the mood. Here's a fun question: how many kids do you want to have?"

"I don't know, haven't thought much about it."

"I want five," she emphatically said.

"Five?" Jim asked with a bit of shock.

"Yeah. I want a big family, and I want to have a special sign with each of them just like you and your mom. Think you could handle five kids?"

"I guess so."

"That would be a lot of soccer games. That'd make me a super soccer mom, wouldn't it?"

He laughed while she moved in to snuggle closely on his lap. His body tingled from the warmth that rolled through his core.

Jim thought to himself, "Wow, this is awesome. Being with a wonderful girl in the park and…"

Sydney interrupted his thoughts. "Can you imagine if you would have met someone else when you first got to Evansville? You could have ended up with some boring girl."

She placed her head back into his lap while she stretched out on the grass in front of him. Closing her eyes, she felt love move from Jim's fingers as he ran them through her hair. A feeling of inner peace swallowed the young couple in the moment. Emotions were strong, as Jim quietly reflected on his true feelings.

"I love you," he quietly whispered with his fingers entangled in her hair.

"What was that?" Sydney said while looking up at Jim.

Tension shot through his body.

"Did I say that out loud?" He questioned himself.

Trying to recover, he replied, "Wait, What? I didn't say anything.

Are you trying to read my thoughts?"

"No, but what are you thinking?" She posed while looking deep into his eyes.

"Nothing much; just enjoying the moment."

"Well," she said with a long, playful tone, "enjoy away."

"Whew, could have blown that one," he thought to himself with relief.

Sydney smiled and snuggled in closer to Jim, thinking about the words he'd most certainly whispered.

"I think I'm in love with you too," she smiled, as she closed her eyes to enjoy the moment.

CHAPTER 47

A FEW DAYS LATER IN the cafeteria, Jim's phone buzzed to life on the table, interrupting a quick lunch between classes with Sydney.

"It's my mom. I'll call her back later."

"No, go ahead and answer it. Maybe it's important," Sydney directed.

Jim eyed the phone for a second before succumbing to her request. He reluctantly slid his finger across the screen and lifted it up to his ear.

"Hey Mom," he said.

"Are you still alive up there?" She asked. "I haven't talked to you in a week."

"Come on, mom. I called you just a couple of days ago. Anyways, I'm doing great."

"I'm sorry, I didn't mean to bother you. Just wanted to say hi, and to see how things are going. You know, I just want to make sure you're doing well at college."

Jim pointed at the phone and rolled his eyes again.

"Mom, come on," he continued with a pinch of obvious frustration. "Things are great, but you sound all depressed or something. I don't know why you're so bummed all the time. The team is two wins away from our first ever conference title, I'm doing great with Sydney, but you sound like I'm on my deathbed or something."

"I didn't mean to sound like that, or to upset you. I just wanted to call you and wish you luck with the game this week."

"I'm not mad. It's just that…"

"It's okay, Jim," she said, cutting him off. "I better get going anyways. I'm going to the hardware store with your father, and he's ready to leave. I'll try calling you another day."

"Sounds good; have fun."

"Bye, son."

"Bye."

Jim hung up the phone and rubbed his hands over his face in frustration. "I hate it when she does that. I think she calls me too much."

"Jim, don't be so hard on her," Sydney said. "You know she just misses you. Think about it, her life completely revolved around you for how many years, and then poof, you're gone."

Through the experience of Sydney's childhood, she certainly understood the importance of loving parents. She had wished her entire life for parents who would have cared about her daily activities, and now she was determined to do everything she could to not be the cause of a strained relationship between Jim and his mother.

Jim hesitated for a moment before responding. "I know. I just wish she would stop with all the guilt trip stuff."

"She will. Just give her time, and keep letting her know you care."

"You're probably right."

"I know I'm right," Sydney said in a teasing tone, through a bite of a peanut butter and banana sandwich. "Stick with me Jim. I will teach you a thing or two about women."

CHAPTER 48

TRADITIONAL SEVENTIES ROCK MUSIC was blaring from Jim's signature game day CD. However, a healthy level of tension seemed to hang in the locker room air. Evansville had not lost a game so far this season, and each passing win seemed to fill the team with a creeping feeling of, "will this be the night?" That evening, they were playing Missouri State—another nationally ranked team, sitting alongside Evansville in the top twenty-five nationally.

Coach Peterson exited his office and signaled to the team. "Bring it in, guys."

The team quickly gathered to an open area in front of the bank of lockers. The coach could easily sense the nerves. Though he loved the focus, he was concerned that his players might play hesitant and tight.

"We only have a few games left in the season," he said. "It feels great to be in first place, doesn't it?"

A few players gave a half-hearted yell in support.

"C'mon guys. This is something to be proud of. Let's hear it!" He yelled again, finally getting his team to roar with life.

"We all know tonight will be tough. Let's go out there and win it. After this game, we only need to win one out of the next four, and we're the conference champs. Tonight, we control our own destiny, men. If we play our style of play and don't let them breathe, we'll come away with the victory."

Coach Peterson paused for a moment, pumped his fist, and yelled, "Let's take it to these guys!"

The team erupted; chest bumps and high-fives circled the room before the players ran out onto the field.

CHAPTER 49

Debbie was getting ready to attend a business dinner with Tom. However, her mind was far away, locked in deep reflection about what was transpiring between her and her son.

When Tom entered the room, he was already dressed for dinner. "Are you all set to go?"

"Oh, I'm sorry, Tom. I'm still getting ready."

Tom could sense there was something going on with his wife.

"Are you sure you want to come to this silly dinner tonight? It's not that important; plus, my boss won't even be there," he lovingly added.

"Tom, I'm sorry. I don't know what has taken over me. Life has just felt so heavy the past little bit; but give me a few minutes, and I'll put on a happy face."

He placed his notebook on the table and tenderly put his arms around his wife.

"I know you're struggling with Jim being gone—we both are. It has been hard for me, too, with him being at Evansville. I think you and I need to just hang onto each other. Trust me, it will get better. I've watched you and Jim for eighteen years, and I have seen firsthand how special your bond with him is. I can promise you that he hasn't forgotten about you; but he is also trying to find out who he is as an independent adult. I hate to be cliché, but he is becoming a man, and I think it is important for us to let him grow."

A few tears rolled down her cheek as she squeezed Tom tight, offering and receiving a reassuring hug.

"I wish I could be happy for him," she said. "I just wish I knew what kind of girl he was falling for. What if she convinces him not to go on a mission, or what if he stops caring about school?"

"Honey, you need to trust your son. We taught him well. He will make good decisions—just give him time. The only way you will get past this, is to have faith that he will do the right thing. I believe in Jim, and I think you need to as well."

She gave Tom another tight squeeze. "I love you so much. I am not sure what I did to deserve a man like you."

"I love you too, my beautiful angel."

Debbie could feel his heartbeat as the two shared their deep devotion with a long embrace and a few tender kisses. Feeling renewed, she said, "I wish I could talk to Jim right now and make things right."

"Well, I assume he's prepping for his game, and I'm sure he doesn't have his phone with him."

"Do you think I could make it for the second half?" She thought out loud.

"What?" Tom asked with confusion. "Maybe the last twenty

minutes or so—it's a bit of a long drive."

She stood up straight, aching to reconcile with her only son. "I really want to try. I really want to make things right with Jim."

"I guess you can give it a try."

Debbie stopped and said, "Honey, no. I'm sorry. Let's go to your dinner. That was really selfish of me."

"No, you're right. Honestly, I think getting things right with Jim is far more important than this dinner. Also, I'm the one who is being selfish. All I want is my happy wife back."

"Seriously, Tom? Are you okay with me skipping the dinner? I would love to try and see Jim after his game tonight, if you are really okay with it."

"Of course I am," Tom said, offering another hug.

With a bit of surprise in her voice, she said, "I'm going to do it."

Tom let go of his wife, patted her on the butt, and said, "Well, hustle up then."

She smiled and hurried to change back into casual clothes.

"Give Jim my love," he said to his wife, in hopes that the negative emotions darkening their home these past few weeks would finally be gone.

Debbie changed clothes, made a sandwich, grabbed her keys, and ran to the car. A kind of peaceful renewal filled her soul as she drove to Evansville. She was making record time and hoped to catch the entirety of the second half. Jim must have felt his mother's connection that night, because his play was spectacular. In the first forty minutes alone, he scored three goals.

Not long into his business dinner, Tom excused himself to get an update on Debbie's progress.

"Hey, Pumpkin, where are you?"

"I'm about fifteen minutes outside of Evansville."

"How you feeling?"

"I'm better; thanks for putting up with my horrible mood."

"Hey, you've put up with me for over twenty years. Plus, you know how I love your lip; how it gets all quivered when you're sad."

"I'm not that obvious, am I?"

"Nooo, not at all," he replied with a good-humored, drawn out sarcastic tone.

"Okay, okay; I get it."

"I've got to go back to this dinner. Call me once the game is over. Jim is going to be so surprised to see you."

"I love you, Tom."

"I love you, too. And please drive safe," Tom ended.

"I will, Tom. I'm feeling good about working everything out. Talk to you soon."

Debbie hung up the phone and realized that she had been so consumed in her thoughts that the radio had been playing only static. She reached into the center console for a CD. Pleasantly surprised, the first one she pulled from the console was the pink, after-game CD that she had made when Jim was young.

"The stars must be aligned tonight," she joked to herself.

That CD would be the perfect soundtrack to help her contemplate all the blessings she had received throughout her life. She looked down at the pink label. Though it had a few nicks and scratches, the it looked as if it was still in fairly good shape--considering it was old and had been played two or three times a week for years.

"I married the most amazing man and I have the most amazing zone," she said out loud as she continued to review the blessings in her life.

Debbie put the CD into the player and reached to put the CD case away, but it hit the side of the console and fell to the floor on the passenger side. Still lost in her thoughts, she leaned over and reached far down to pick up the case. She swept her hand around on the floor mat, taking her eyes off the road for just a second to locate the case.

When she eventually looked up, her heart leapt. A deer, frozen with fear, stood directly in the path of her car. Instinctively, she swerved to the left to avoid slamming into the frightened animal. The car pulled hard and threw her into oncoming traffic. Debbie's eyes opened wide as she cut the steering wheel hard to the right in an attempt to move back into her lane. The car veered back across the road, but she was losing control and quickly realized that fighting the wheel was futile; her fate was sealed. The car careened off the right side of the road, its head lights focusing her attention on the large oak tree that was rapidly filling up the view of her windshield.

At that instant, Debbie's mind shot back in time to a vision of her son swinging on the tire that hung from a mighty oak tree in their backyard. Tears welled in her eyes as she remembered Little J's joyous smile radiating with each gentle push of her hand. She had pushed him on that swing for hours. During his childhood sickness, some days it had been the only thing that would get him out of the house. Eventually, their time together had led to him discovering soccer.

Immediately, the violent shaking of her car careening off the side of the road brought her back to reality as the distance between the car and the tree closed.

Debbie let go of the wheel and whispered, "Dead God, please watch over my son."

Everything went black.

CHAPTER 50

THE FIRST FEW VIBRATIONS of Jim's phone did little to spark his interest. He was partying with his friends after the big win and had no desire to spend any time on the phone. He truly cherished time with his teammates, and with Sydney.

Jim, answer the phone.

He was incredibly startled by this unspoken command.

Had it been a whisper? No, it couldn't have been. The restaurant was far too loud for anyone to hear a whisper. The voice had been in his head, or heart, or soul—it had been something powerful, but he couldn't figure out what it had been. Panic swept over him, so overwhelming that his body became numb. He slipped his hand into his pocket, and he pulled out his phone. He looked at the screen and saw it was lit up with an incoming call.

"Hey guys, it's my dad. Just give me a sec," he said while standing up from the table.

Sydney had no interest in the conversation at the table. She thought it was a little unusual for Jim to take a call at that time. He had always been the old fashioned, gentlemanly type. When they were together, they'd had an unwritten rule to try and not answer their phones. However, she, too, was overcome by a strange feeling, which was confirmed when she saw the blood drain from Jim's face. She jumped to her feet and ran to him. He was obviously losing all semblance of consciousness.

"Jim, what's going on?" She said in a panic.

His face glazed with shock and his hand fell limp, causing the cell phone to crash to the floor. The distinct clatter of circuitry on the linoleum caused everyone around them to turn in Jim's direction. His lifeless eyes stared off into the distance, pain filling them with a sorrowful liquid.

"What's up, bro?" Lance jumped up to solicit.

Jim shifted his gaze towards his friend. The void in his face told Lance all he needed to know—tragedy was in the air. Suddenly, Jim sprang to life, dashed towards the door, and threw it open with all his might. He ran across the parking lot and flung himself into his car. With the unsettling screech of tires, he drove his car around the corner, rushing onto the main road.

Lance turned towards Sydney and yelled, "What's going on?"

"I don't know?" She cried in response, panic racing through her mind.

She looked down at the floor and saw the screen on Jim's phone was still lit up. She quickly reached down and picked it up, checked the call history, and saw that the incoming call was from Jim's father. Jim's reaction had been so startling; she could only image what had been said.

She and Lance instinctively grabbed their stuff and ran to Lance's sports car. They sped off from the parking lot with an equally loud squeal. They made it onto the road just in time to see Jim's tail lights in the distance. Lance gave everything his car could handle. After fifteen minutes and a couple of broken laws, the pair eventually caught up to Jim, as he was pulling in front of the hospital. Lance barely had time to bring the car to a stop before Sydney jumped out and ran into the building.

Jim rushed to the reception desk and frantically demanded, "Debbie Anderson?"

The receptionist acted as if she hadn't heard him and continued typing on her keyboard. Jim violently slammed his fists on the counter, causing her to physically jump back in fear.

"Debbie Anderson! She just came in on an ambulance," he screamed in the woman's face.

The blank stare on the receptionist's face was enough for Jim to know that she would be no help. He began to search the small hospital himself. Finally, through a small glass window, he spotted two doctors and a number of support staff frantically working on someone. He gasped for breath as he immediately recognized the floral-print shoes lying on the floor—last year's Mother's Day gift from him.

He pressed his hands and face right up to the glass and could now clearly see his mother lying motionless on the table. Tears rolled down his face and panic filled his heart as he watched the frantic scene take place before him. He moved to the door and pushed it open.

"I'm sorry, we can't allow anyone in the triage room," one of the nurses said as she walked towards Jim.

"But that's my mom," Jim protested.

The nurse reassured, "Okay, I understand. Can I have you wait outside while the doctors work? Everything will be okay."

Jim paused for a moment. He wanted to be by his mother's side but also trusted the nurse's reassuring voice. He decided to allow the doctors to work uninterrupted and returned to the window outside the operating room.

Sydney and Lance, having arrived only seconds behind their friend, watched from a short distance away. Jim could only see glimpses of his mother, as the doctors moved around her body, frantically trying to perform a miracle. Purple bruising was visible on Debbie's face, and her hair was matted with blood and glass. Her mangled right hand drooped off the edge of the table, and blood dripped on the floor of her limp pinky. Her right leg was also visible and twisted in a very unnatural way.

"Oh God, please save her," Jim whispered in prayer. "God, I am pleading with you. Please!"

His hand was pressed against the glass, his fingers slowly sliding down with each minute that past, a sense of the inevitable setting in. Sydney grabbed his arm, offering her support, while she and Lance stepped next to Jim and stared into the room.

Waiting.

Hoping for any positive signs.

It seemed as if an eternity had passed—in reality, it was only a few minutes—before the frantic pace inside the triage room began to slow. The lead surgeon lowered his head, moved away from the table, and began to remove his gloves. Debbie lay motionless on the table, as the nurses also moved away.

"What's going on?" Jim turned to Sydney, hoping that as he looked back into the room he would realize this was all fiction and that his mother would stand up and walk toward them, perfectly unharmed.

He knew the truth, though.

He just didn't want to accept it.

"No!" He screamed, breaking away from Sydney's side.

He crashed through the triage room doors, startling the doctors and nurses. He rushed forward and forcefully grabbed the doctor by his operating gown.

Jim screamed in his face. "Why are you stopping? You can't stop! Fix her!"

He was desperate. The doctor tried to pull away, but Jim was holding on with every sinew of his being. All the doctor could do was look at him with fear. The muscles in Jim's well-trained arms were bulging with rage. But the doctor knew from experience that she was gone.

Seeing the certainty in the doctor's eyes, Jim was flushed with disbelief. He shoved the surgeon back towards the operating table.

"Call security!" The surgeon screamed as he fell to the floor and partially slid in his patient's blood.

Jim slammed his hands against his own head. The internal pain was overwhelming. He had to do something; and instantly he thought of something that might work. He rapidly moved towards the bed and knelt down on the floor. He slowly reached forward and grabbed his mother's mangled hand from where it was hanging down from the operating table. He gently grabbed her soft, lifeless fingers and tried to shape them into their special hand sign. Painfully positioning her fingers into a half heart, he desperately pushed his free hand against hers. With each attempt, her broken fingers remained limp, as a few drops of blood fell into his lap.

"Please! Mom, please!" He cried each time he linked their hands together.

Jim finally stood up and looked at his mother's face. He didn't see the blood, glass, and bruising. All his saw before his eyes was a flood of images of soccer games and car rides. And then it happened, a sudden memory flashed into his mind—his impossible memory.

Jim sprang to life as he reached forward and grabbed his mother around her neck and legs. He easily lifted her petite body off the table, but in his frantic pace, her bare foot knocked over a tray of bloody surgical equipment and the IV still attached to her arm began to topple the monitoring machine. The crash of stainless steel startled everyone in the room, except him. With a rapid motion he sat down on the floor against the wall, with his mother in his lap, and burst into tears.

"Don't worry, mom. We'll make it through the night. I'm holding you; we'll make it through the night. I'm here as long as it takes. We'll make it through the night."

Lance and Sydney, as tears streamed down their faces, were overcome by the scene.

The nurses in the room were doing all they could to hold in their emotions. They had never seen such a visceral reaction before. The special connection between mother and son was evident, as was how death's omnipotent sting was tearing that bond apart. The tragic reality of the situation swept over Lance. His mind froze with fear and uncertainty over how to react in this situation. He slowly surveyed the room.

Sydney was standing softly in the corner, tear-soaked hands covering her mouth. Watching a deluge of emotions rip through Jim like a tsunami, she was in a shock-like state and had no idea what to do next. Jim's ravaged, tear-stained eyes squeezed tight as he held his mom in his arms. He screamed out, his head turned heavenward, and he cursed his very Maker. No one in the room could escape the moment—a loving son facing the reality of his mother's sudden passing. All anyone could do was wipe away tears of their own and bow their heads in silent reverence.

A loud bang startled everyone as Tom frantically entered the room, out of breath and distraught. The harsh scene took hold as he eyes focused on his eternal love, lying lifeless in his son's lap. Frozen with fear, he stood in horror with the realization that it was too late. His wife had passed without a goodbye. Tom dropped to his knees and ran his hand tenderly across her forehead and down to her chin. He sobbed bitterly, trying to wipe the tangled hair and blood from her face.

Jim reached forward and grabbed his father's hand.

Tom lifted his head and looked into his son's gaze—a darkness was all that was left, where a sparkle had once shone.

CHAPTER 51

OVER THE NEXT FOUR days, Jim never returned to campus and chose to seal himself inside his bedroom at home.

He wanted to be alone; he wanted to hurt. His days were spent swinging wildly between deep resentment and bitter hopelessness. Weeping uncontrollably was a frighteningly common occurrence. Only focusing on the negative, he bounced around between thoughts of how he had spent all his time with Sydney and missed the last few months with his mother. If he had only known.

"Where was the comfort God had promised?" Frequently crossed his mind.

He prayed often. However, he witnessed no angels. He heard no still, small voice. He felt no warmth at all. At times, he would just lie on his bed and stare at the cold ceiling, filled with silence—ugly, soul-ripping silence. Tom was hardly any better, haunted by his own unbearable grief. He'd had every intention of being the man of the house and helping his son deal with the loss. However, all he could occasionally muster was the strength to exit his own room, knock on Jim's door, and ask how his son was doing. Silence had been the typical response, smattered with the occasional blast of, "leave me alone."

As it always does, time marched forward and the day arrived for the two, broken men to place their most prized loved one in the ground. Tom did his best to make the service and graveside ceremony a low-key affair. But, with Jim's fame and the tragic nature of the accident, Tom's efforts were unsuccessful. An overflowing crowd gathered at the chapel and accompanied the family to the gravesite. Jim hung tight by his father's side. He displayed the emotional countenance of the granite stone that his mother's name would be carved into. There were no more tears left to shed.

Sydney had not seen or communicated with Jim since the accident. Although she had hardly known Debbie, her death had taken quite a toll on Sydney as well. She desperately wanted to be with Jim, but he wouldn't let her. She had texted him and called the Anderson home so many times, she feared her insistence had bordered on harassment. It hadn't been just with Sydney; Jim had refused to talk to anyone.

During the graveyard service, she tactfully pushed her way to the front of the guests and stood directly across from him. The only thing separating the two was the shiny metal of the closed casket. Sydney was determined to make contact with him, and, as macabre as it might have seemed, the funeral was her best opportunity.

Lance, Coach Peterson, and the rest of Jim's teammates were also in attendance. Jim was their leader, and it struck most of them to the very core to see his eyes so lifeless—almost infinitely void. The service was short and very raw. Tom and Jim's pain was very real and it tore at the hearts of all those present. Silence surrounded the mourners as they watched the father and son say their last goodbyes. At the conclusion of the service, Tom put his arm around Jim and whispered, "God will carry us through this."

Jim hesitated for a moment and angrily snapped back, "Yeah, just like He was there for mom?"

Tom was shaken. What had happened to his son? The sudden lack of faith had been rapid. Tom wanted to council his son, but immediately following the graveside service was certainly not the time. He gently absorbed the comment and kept their focus on his dear wife. He slowly removed his arm from around Jim and walked alone back to the limousine that had transported them from the church to the cemetery.

Sydney had seen Tom and Jim's confrontation. She had been too far away to hear what had been said between the father and son. However, Jim was now alone and she realized this might be her best chance to catch him. Approaching from behind, she lightly placed both her hands on his shoulders. She wanted to provide comfort; to be the person to rescue Jim from the awful pit of despair into which he had clearly fallen.

"Jim?" She quietly asked. "I want to be here for you. What I can I do to help?"

Jim's soul wanted to turn around, embrace Sydney, and find his way home again. However, his body was not there yet. Pain and prideful anger had taken full control. He intentionally made no motion in her direction and began walking towards the limousine.

"Jim, please. I love you," she pleaded in the direction of his unabashed stride toward the vehicle.

The message had been crystal clear; he did not want to talk to her. She stopped and agonizingly felt as if Jim were walking out of her life without even batting an eye. He marched steadily towards the parking lot.

This time, Tom was the witness. Through the dark tint of the limousine's window, he watched Sydney break down. His heart rent with compassion.

"I know he is hurting, but how could Jim treat her like that?" He questioned.

Sydney sat on the grass with her head buried in her hands. She could not hold in her sorrow any longer, and it all spilled out. After a few minutes of heavy sobs, she felt a loving hand on her left shoulder. She looked up and saw the caring eyes of Tom looking down on her. After his son's disrespectful display, he had gotten out of the limo and walked towards Sydney.

He sat down and tenderly whispered in her ear, "It'll be okay."

"What can I do?" She pleaded through the tears.

He kindly wrapped his arm around her shoulders, as if she were his own daughter. He gave her a loving squeeze and spoke softly. "It will all be okay. Just have faith in Jim. He's a good man, and he'll make it through this."

Sydney could see the love in Tom's eyes, and a glimmer of peace fluttered across her soul. The pair remained on the grass releasing the pain they held inside. Tears were flowing, and a slow healing was taking place.

Across the cemetery in the parking lot, Jim glared with disdain.

CHAPTER 52

THE LOCKER ROOM PRIOR to the following night's home game was subdued. Since the accident, Jim had not been seen on campus, nor at practice. Lance was the only person who had actually talked with him. He had gained enough trust during their short friendship that he had finally been able to contact Jim. The somber mood in the locker room made it difficult for the players to focus on the game.

"Jim playing?" Adriel asked Lance, while they were getting dressed.

"I don't know. I talked to him this morning, and he said he was coming."

As if by some predetermined cue, Jim quietly entered the room and approached his locker. He stared straight ahead as he made his way across the room, grabbed his lock, and began turning the dial, entering the code.

"How you doing?" Lance asked with a subdued voice as he leaned against the locker next to Jim's.

"I'm fine."

"Are you sure you want to suit up? I mean, it would…"

"Yeah, I'm fine," Jim responded with his eyes intentionally focused on his locker.

Lance ended by simply patting him on the back. "See you out there, brother."

Lance grabbed his equipment bag and headed onto the field with the rest of the team. The drab mood in the locker room seemed to follow the team. In fact, everyone in the stadium could sense it. The team was very somber, and their usual high-energy pre-game warm up was absent. Jim had decided not to head out to the field with the team and decided to stay in the locker room.

Not knowing if she would see Jim or not, Sydney had decided to attend the game as well. As she found a seat on the third row, her phone buzzed. Her body tingled as she read a short text from Lance. "He's here."

When Jim finally exited the locker room, the entire crowd rose to their feet and gave him a respectful standing ovation. Yet, he did little to acknowledge the gesture. He simply placed his bag on the ground and began to stretch. The opening whistle eventually blew and the game began. An uneasiness was in the air, as if playing soccer was just not the right thing to be doing that night. A few minutes into the game, Adriel made an errant pass back towards his goalie. An opposing player easily stole the ball, dribbled in front of the goal, and scored.

Jim went berserk.

"What kind of pass was that?" He screamed at Adriel. "We can't afford that crap in our own end. Why don't you just tee it up for him next time?"

Adriel, who was certainly not one to back down from a fight, stood his ground while Jim approached and screamed, "There are no excuses for that kind of play. You're doing nothing on the field but making us loose."

The two continued to scream at each other as they bumped chests in anger. Lance bolted over and got in between the two before anything more serious happened. Jim forcefully ripped his arm from Lance's grip and headed to the middle of the field, mumbling in frustration.

"Just ignore him and keep playing," Lance said to Adriel before trotting off.

The balance of the game grew increasingly tense. Players on both sides became uncomfortable with Jim's agitation, and the end of the match could not have come soon enough. Thankfully, the whistle finally blew and the opposing team cheered with exuberance. Evansville, the top ranked team in the nation, had just been beat. The Evansville players collectively hung their heads low and slowly gathered their equipment bags.

"Tough loss," Lance said while walking next to Jim.

"Yah think?"

"You okay, man?"

"No, Lance, I'm not. We just lost to one of the worst teams in the conference. Our first loss of the season, may I remind you. I don't even know why I chose to play with you guys at this crappy school."

"Ease up a bit, man. Everyone's feeling for you, but you're not making this easy for us."

Jim abruptly stopped and turned to face Lance.

"What? Without me on this team, you would lose every single game. I'm not going to ease up. You know what? Why don't you carry my bag," he said before throwing his bag at Lance's feet.

Lance stood still for a moment, fuming inside, but he steadied himself to figure out his next move. His gut told him to grab Jim by the back of the neck and knock him to the ground. Luckily, Lance's cooler head prevailed. He picked up Jim's bag and made his way to the locker room.

CHAPTER 53

THE NEXT WEEK, JIM made his first trip back to regular classes. Around noon, he found a park bench and sat alone to eat a sandwich. Sydney was walking to her second class of the day and spotted him across the way. She hoped he would finally let her in. Again, she walked up from behind and placed her soft hands over his eyes.

"Guess who?" She said with a playful tone.

To her surprise and disappointment, Jim forcefully pushed her hands off his face.

"Jim, I'm really concerned about you."

"Why?" He coldly responded.

"C'mon," she quietly pleaded, moving around the bench to sit beside him. "I'm really trying here. You know I love you very much"

"Stop!" He said with force.

"Stop what?"

"Stop trying."

"We have something special, and I want to be there for you. Isn't that what your mother would have wanted for us?"

"You have no idea what my mother would have wanted," he said. "You have no idea about me or my family at all, so stop pretending."

"I know that, Jim. But I'm trying, and I have to start somewhere. Look, I'm grieving for your mom, the same as you."

He rose from the bench with fury and turned to face her.

"You're grieving for my mom?" He yelled in her face. "You're grieving for a lady you barely knew. Well, good for you."

He paused as tears began to well up in Sydney's eyes. Veins were visibly pulsating in his neck. He continued. "You know what? Maybe it would have been better if we had never met. You know my mother was coming down that night because of you, right?"

"Jim, please don't do this. Please don't say that," she pleaded.

"Don't beg Sydney; you look pathetic."

He stormed off, leaving Sydney sitting on the bench, demolished as if a bulldozer had just crushed her heart.

CHAPTER 54

OVER THE NEXT FEW days, Tom stayed home feeling like his entire day was unfocused. If he managed to pull himself out of bed each morning, he considered that day a success. On campus, Jim was continuing to attend classes. However, he was paying little attention to the lectures going on around him, or the homework assignments that were piling up past due. He was just going through the motions.

With only three games left on the soccer schedule, his upcoming game landed on the next Friday night. The pre-game mood in the locker room was cold. Lance knew he had to do something and took it upon himself to get the team fired up. After a season of using the locker next to Jim's, Lance knew his lock combination. He quickly opened up his teammate's locker, pulled out the psyche CD, popped it into the boom box, and cranked up the volume. The change in the atmosphere wasn't dramatic, but the music certainly helped to lighten the mood before the important game.

Almost as rapidly as the room loosened up, it instantly zipped tight again when Jim entered through the back door. The entire team stared at him, waiting to see what would happen next. Jim immediately cruised over to the boom box and pulled the CD from the player. The music instantly stopped, leaving an eerie silence hanging in the air.

"What?" Lance asked uncomfortably.

"Where'd you get this?"

"From your locker. I just thought it would help us get ready for the game."

He walked over to Lance and got right up into his face. "Stay out of my stuff."

Jim put the CD back into the case and tossed it into his equipment bag. He looked around at the rest of his teammates with a defiant stare.

"Well, that didn't go according to plan," Lance thought.

Unfortunately, the scene in the locker room was only an omen of things to come. When the players quietly exited the locker to warm up for the game, the feeling in the stadium was once more subdued. However, ten minutes into the first half, Jim's play became more aggressive than ever before, and the mood in the stadium began to pick up. At first, this aggression served as motivation for his teammates. The Evansville team's level of play improved to match Jim's intensity, and they took an early one-to-zero lead. Everyone began to see the spark return to Jim's eyes. It may have been too early to tell during the first half of the game, but it seemed as if a few smiles had crept across his face.

As with every prior match this season, the opposing team knew that Jim was the key to an Evansville victory. Every move he made was hotly contested. All night, he was shadowed by an opposing team's defender, who would push, pull, and hold on to Jim's jersey, at times to ensure that his movements weren't free.

After the first forty-five minutes of play, it became clear to the opposing coaching staff that the only chance for winning the game was to take Jim out of it. As the second half began, his shadow defender brought out some dirty play, eventually leading to a spat after a hard tackle that had not gone unnoticed by the referee.

The ref ran over to the pair and broke up the exchange of words. Reaching into his pocket, he issued both Jim and his opposing defender a yellow card.

"Did you see his elbow, ref?" The defender screamed in defense.

Jim countered, "Cut your whining. You're a big boy,"

The ref broke in. "Both of you, settle down, or in the near future you will be seeing a red card."

As play resumed, Jim and his shadow continued to aggressively jockey for position; neither had any intention of being outmaneuvered by the other. On multiple occasions, the defender grabbed Jim by the shirt and held him back.

"C'mon mamma's boy. Is that all you got?" The defender spewed.

This verbal jab hit Jim deep in the gut. Immediately, he swung around to face the opposing player—their faces only inches apart.

The defender screamed in Jim's face, "C'mon man, take a swing." It took all of Jim's restraint to keep his emotions in check.

"Too scared, huh?" The defender taunted. "It's 'cause mommy can't save you now,' can she? I guess six feet of dirt will keep anyone down."

That was it.

All semblance of rational thought was gone, and primal instincts took control. Jim's muscles violently contracted. Every emotion he had felt over the last two weeks exploded to the surface. Rage seemed as if it were spewing from every pore. He lunged toward the unsuspecting player with a thundering shove to the chest, knocking him to the ground. Jim's fists clinched with fury, and his eyes were on fire. He pounced like a cornered lion onto his stumbling foe. He cocked his arm back and released the grief he'd kept bottled inside. The swing of his arm was fast, flying towards the other player's face. The defenseless player desperately put his arms up to deflect the blow, sending Jim's heavy fist into the dirt.

Shocked by what he was witnessing, Lance sprinted to intervene. Without slowing, he jumped midair and tackled Jim off the helpless opponent. Jim was frantic, violently pushing Lance away as their bodies tumbled across the grass. As Lance quickly tried to regain his balance, the rest of the Evansville team intervened, pinning Jim to ground. Jim tried to pull his arms away and rise to his feet, but he could not break free. With the force of a Spartan warrior, he let out a piercing scream, spit disgorging from his mouth.

The crowd watched in stunned silence as the fight took place on the field. A number of opposing players quickly attended to their teammate, while a few jawed and egged on the fight. The opposing player rolled over onto his stomach. Moaning from Jim's blow to his chest, he tried to push himself onto his elbows. Only a short distance away, Jim was wild with anger. Mud and blades of grass covered his face while his teammates held him to the ground.

"Get off me," he screamed. "I'll kill him."

With the side of his head still pinned to the grass by Lance's muscular forearm, Jim caught a glimpse of the player who'd started it all. He jerked and struggled, trying to break free.

"I'll kill you!" He screamed. "You're a dead man. You hear me?"

Both coaches were on the field trying to restore order, as the situation spun wildly out of control. The referee was in as much shock as everyone else. He stood silently, watching Jim's teammates attempting to keep him on the ground.

The opposing coach grabbed the ref by the arm and screamed, "You better get security, and get that kid out of here."

"Just call the game," Coach Peterson yelled as the ref approached.

The ref quickly nodded his head in approval, blew his whistle, and waved his arms in the air. Evansville immediately forfeited the game. A much-needed victory for the home team vanished. The opposition quickly grabbed their equipment and ran off the field. The spectators stood dumbfounded, eyes fixed on the still-ongoing battle to restrain Jim.

CHAPTER 55

THE NEXT DAY, A tense silence hung inside Tom's car as he drove Jim to the athletic building, where he was to meet with Coach Peterson. Upon arrival, Jim exited the car, opened the door to the building, and walked in; all without a backwards glance toward his father. When he arrived at Coach Peterson's office, the coach was sitting behind his desk reading the local newspaper.

"Jim," he said while folding the paper and placing it under a notebook. "Have a seat."

Jim slid into the cold metal chair on the opposite side of the desk. He was embarrassed. He was upset. He just wanted some peace and didn't know how to find it. He struggled to look his coach in the eye.

Coach Peterson, on the other hand, was experienced. He was ready to tackle the issue head on—no sugarcoating required. "I'm sure you've heard—you're suspended. You're lucky it's just one game. I almost figured the NCAA might be pressuring me to suspend you for the rest of the season."

"That's what they should've done," Jim said, still unable to look at his coach.

"Is that what you really want?" Coach Peterson paused to collect his thoughts. He wanted to ensure that he chose his words carefully. "You know, son, Evansville wouldn't be at the top of the polls without you. Everyone understands that. It's clear as day. You know, I'm just sick inside about what happened with your mother. I wish I could stop the world today, right now, and let all the wounds heal. But I don't have that luxury."

Jim finally looked up at his coach.

"I have a responsibility to all twenty players on this team. I have a special responsibility to our nine seniors. I'm empathetic for all that has happened to you, but you and I need to talk about your future on this team."

"I told you. I'm done."

Coach Peterson paused and thought for a moment. "Then, why are you still here?"

No movement from Jim.

"I want you to go home for a week. Get away from campus. I've talked to your teachers and your dad, and we all agree this would be the best option for you."

Jim hung his head, slightly confused and insolent.

"We have a road game next, and then our last game at home is against Loyola. As you know, they are currently neck-and-neck with us, fighting for the conference title. It'll be a battle. I only want you back for that last game, if you are one-hundred-percent ready. Do we have a deal?"

Jim nodded his head with a silent shrug before exiting the room.

Coach Peterson truly ached for him. From having coached hundreds of kids over a twenty-year career, he had gained very thick skin. But this situation with Jim was different. The young man's talent was remarkable, and his emotions were intense.

Tom had planned on going in with Jim, but the abruptness with which Jim left the car had let Tom know that he was not welcome. Waiting in the car, he saw Jim exit the building and drove over to pick him up.

"How'd it go?" He inquired.

"Let's just get my stuff from my room and get out of here."

The pair drove to Jim's dorm. It took only a couple of minutes for Jim to grab a handful of clothes and his soccer gear. He hastily threw his stuff into the back of the car and slammed the door. Tom started the engine, and to two broken men began the drive home.

"You've got a good coach," said Tom, attempting to break the silence.

Jim made no attempt to acknowledge his father's comment.

The disappointment Tom felt in his son deepened. With all that had happened, he could only take so much. His temper was quickly reaching its boiling point. He had been extremely patient, but Jim's pride and anger had reached unacceptable levels.

"You know, son, this behavior will only serve to make your life worse."

No response from Jim.

"You're pretty lucky you weren't suspended for the entire year. I'm guessing they went a little easy on you, because of mom's passing."

"That kid is lucky I didn't kill him," Jim barked in return.

"No, son," Tom responded in a demanding tone, just degrees away from reaching his true boiling point. "As I see it, you're the lucky one. He could have pressed charges. I talked to his parents to make sure he was going to be okay. They were very understanding and, quite frankly, very forgiving, considering how viciously you went after their son."

"Honestly Dad, I don't really care," Jim dismissively replied.

Tom took a moment to collect his thoughts and tried to keep his voice low. "So, is this how it's going to be at home? It's easy when everything's going your way, isn't it? But a real man shows what he's made of by the way he responds when his chips are down."

"Thanks for the sermon, but, as I so astutely stated before, I really don't care."

Tom was not deterred by the sarcasm.

"It comes down to this," he reasoned. "Are you strong enough to stand with character, when everything around you begins to fail, and your soul aches for relief? Or, will you be lost in the dark fog of anger—revenge—like a man with little faith?"

Jim looked at his father for a moment before reaching into his pocket and pulling out the headphones attached to his cell phone. He placed the white ear buds in his ears, selected a song from the screen, and closed his eyes.

"Message received," Tom thought to himself.

Further conversation was futile at this point. Jim's mind was closed.

CHAPTER 56

EVEN THOUGH IT HAD been almost two weeks since Debbie's death, life at the Anderson home had not changed much. Jim continued to spend most of his time alone in his room. On occasion after dinner, he would join his father in the family room to watch a little television. To Tom, having a light conversation with his son about a sitcom or dumb reality show was at least some level of progress. They never talked about Debbie, or soccer. Tom had been able to mask his emotions when Jim was around. He had developed a strong sense of protection for his son and would go to the end of the earth to ensure that Jim made it through this ordeal. Tom felt it was what his dear wife would have wanted. Still, he, too, was overcome with grief and loneliness. Debbie had been his one and only true love—she had been his life. Each day, he struggled to find the strength to rise, but he did it anyway out of the remarkable love for his son.

Evansville's first game without their star player ended with a crushing two-to-one loss. Without Jim on the front line, scoring opportunities were hard to come by. Just four weeks prior, Evansville had had a lock on the conference title and a bid as the top seed to the NCAA national tournament. To ensure the title, the team now had to win their last regular season home game the following Friday.

That night's game was against one of the worst teams in the division and should have been an easy win for Evansville. However, without Jim, the team's play had been disorganized and seemingly unmotivated. A few hours after the loss, Jim's cell phone rang with a call from Lance.

"Hey, Lance," he answered.

"How's it going?"

"I'm hanging in there. I'm a little bored, but okay."

"What about your old man? How's he doing?"

"I don't know. I don't talk to him much. I'm ready to come back and play."

"No kidding. We need you back."

"I'm not sure Coach will let me play again, though."

"Jim, you really think coach would sit you out? Your suspension's over."

"Well, I told him I'm done; never going to play soccer again."

"I think every person on planet earth knows you weren't being serious. You knew you didn't mean it, even as you were saying it."

"True," Jim laughed, realizing how silly it sounded now.

A little bit of life seemed to be returning.

Jim said with a slight smile, "So, I didn't hear anything about the game. Were you finally able to score a goal?"

"As a matter of fact, I did."

"No way; that's awesome," Jim said, with the most amount of positive emotion he had shown since his mother's death.

"Yeah, and I tried to carry the team on my back like you, but fell a little short. We lost the game."

Jim was suddenly filled with competitive spirit. "I thought you said you scored. You let them score on us, too? You realize that we have to win next week, or the title is lost."

"You know—you're lucky you got a roommate who puts up with all your crap."

They both laughed.

Lance felt like the mood had lightened up, so he took a gamble. "Now quit moping around and get your butt back to campus."

The words hung in the air. Lance felt as if he had just taken a forty-yard shot on goal, and the ensuing silence was deafening.

"You're right," Jim said. "I need to get out of this house. Let me talk to my dad and Coach Peterson. I'm sure I'll be back before the end of the week."

Lance hung up the phone, encouraged by the ray of sunshine that seemed to be breaking through that night.

CHAPTER 57

THE DAY BEFORE THE big game, Loyola arrived at the Evansville campus. As they walked off the bus, Coach Peterson was there to greet them and direct them to the visiting locker-room. Sydney watched through a window on the library's fourth floor. She'd been trying to complete some math homework, but had been far more interested in spying on the Loyola players as they gathered their bags. Her days of having a bubbly, over the top demeanor were gone. During the past few weeks, she had tried to come to grips with the train wreck that had plowed through her life.

"Hey," a loud voice said from behind her, causing her to jump.

Turning around and finding the source of the voice to be Bryant, she said, "Oh, you scared me."

He laughed while plopping himself into the seat next to her. "How's it going?"

"Okay, I guess. I haven't seen you in a while."

"Math, huh?" He asked while pointing toward her textbook.

"Yeah; not my best subject."

"Mine, neither."

After a short, awkward silence he asked, "You coming to the big game tomorrow?"

"No, I don't think so."

"What?" He yelled, disturbing the others who were legitimately trying to study. "You have to. This game is it. It's for the division title."

"I can't," she replied with a more serious tone.

"Look, you don't even have to watch the game. You can just come to be a part of the crazy crowd if you want."

She hesitated for a moment. "I'll think about it, but don't count on me."

Bryant smiled, slapped the table, and got up.

"Tomorrow, seven o'clock," he commanded, in another not-so-library-approved voice.

Sydney could feel her face turn a little red because of Bryant's boisterous antics, though they did bring a smile to her face as she waved goodbye to him.

CHAPTER 58

THE FOLLOWING DAY WAS beautiful. A crisp blue sky and a penetrating orange sun made for the perfect afternoon. Jim called Coach Peterson that morning to let him know he would be playing.

"I'm excited to watch you play tonight," Tom said, as he and Jim made the drive to Evansville.

Jim only muttered a muted, "Yep."

"Are you nervous?"

"Not really."

Tom paused for a moment. He had never been good at motivational speeches—they just weren't in his nature. However, the mood felt right, and he knew he needed to attempt to fill the emotional void left by Debbie's passing.

"Jim, tonight you need to find strength in your teammates, not in the circumstance. This has been the worst thing ever for both of us. But if there is one thing I know for certain, it's that there is a tremendous purpose for your life. We are running on empty right now, but I know God has a plan for you and will help you find your way. You just have to figure out what that is." He quietly thought for a moment before resuming, "Once you do figure it out, life won't seem so unbearable."

Jim continued to stare out the window. Tom wasn't sure if his son was contemplating the advice he had just given, or if Jim was just watching the telephone poles whiz by.

"Maybe that was too much," he thought to himself. "Maybe I need to tone it down a bit."

"Just do your best, Son. I'll always love you, no matter the outcome."

"Just cut the speech, dad," Jim said sharply.

Tom reached forward and turned up the radio; he was out of things to say. The two said nothing more for the rest of the drive. Upon their arrival at campus, Jim entered the locker room. He was unsure of how his teammates would react when they saw him again. To his surprise, the room was upbeat. Rap music was pumping through the speakers. In truth, Jim was actually annoyed that his teammates seemed to be having a good time while he was still so torn up inside. Nonetheless, he bottled his feelings and walked over to his locker in silence.

Lance said, "Great to see you, Bro. You ready to win this thing?"

"Not sure."

Jim's tentative answer was not what Lance had hoped for. Sitting on the adjacent bench, Adriel watched their interaction. He had been quite vocal during the past week that he felt it was a bad idea for Jim to be playing. Tonight would be the last home game of Adriel's collegiate career. He was intense and incredibly focused. This was his curtain call, and he didn't want an emotionally unstable guy sucking the air out of the team. He was frustrated with everyone tip-toeing around Jim and treating him as if he were some kind of fragile baby.

Adriel thought to himself, "Not tonight—not going to let this guy ruin our chance of winning this thing."

Without thinking, Adriel swooped to Jim's side, twisting him around. "Hey man, we need you full on tonight. Otherwise, don't take a step out on that field."

Jim was surprised by the action and pulled his arm free from Adriel's grip.

"I'm serious," Adriel barked while grabbing Jim's arm again, to make certain he had the guy's full attention. "If you're not one-hun-dred-percent ready to play, don't dress. We don't need you losing it again. I want to win."

"You want to win, huh?" Jim spouted back. "Well, you better learn some defense, since it sounds like the last couple of games you've just let everyone score."

"Chump, we don't need your crap tonight," Adriel said in frus-tration. He let go of Jim's arm and waved him away. "Why don't you just crawl back home? You're nothing but a weakling and a liability."

Lance broke in, "Hey, ease off man."

Adriel had no intention of backing off. He had a point to make, and he was going to make it.

"No way!" He said to Lance. "This is it for you and me and the other seniors. This is our last year, and I'm not going to let some spoiled freshman ruin it, because he can't man up and face life." He looked right at Jim. "News flash for you, people die. Welcome to life on the streets–my life."

"Adriel, you're way out of line." Lance responded.

"Nah, why don't you stop babying him," Adriel responded before turning towards Jim. "Be a man. You think you're some kind of leader or something."

Jim was fuming. He tried to gain control of himself, but he was finding himself unsuccessful. "You want leadership? We'll you're already the leader," he said while pushing his finger into the captain armband on Adriel's arm. "And with you in charge, I guarantee we'll lose by ten goals."

Lance quickly jumped in front of Adriel to hold him back, staying the impending fist fight. "Knock it off—both of you," he commanded. "We've got a game in thirty minutes and we need you both."

Adriel yelled back at Lance with animation, "You going to let him blow it for us?"

"Screw you!" Jim screamed.

"Screw you, man. My daddy went and got shot up on the streets when I was three. All I've ever had is my momma, and you don't see me boo-hooin' like a little girl. Man up or sit out."

Coach Peterson had heard the ruckus and came crashing out of his office. "What's going on?"

The locker room got deathly quiet, while the coach surveyed the players who had gathered around the commotion. Coach Peterson sternly ordered, "Okay, everyone on the field right now and warm up."

One by one, the team picked up their equipment bags and headed to the field with a tinge of uneasiness. Jim moved towards his locker. He was stopped by a strong hand on his shoulder.

"You stay here," Coach Peterson directed.

Jim stood with a baffled look as the balance of the team quietly exited.

"Sit this one out tonight."

"What? You can't beat Loyola without me, and you know it."

"Then I guess we'll just have to lose," Coach Peterson confidently responded. "I told you on the phone, one-hundred-percent or stay home. This is not one-hundred-percent, so you're not playing tonight."

Jim pulled his shoulder out from under his coach's hand and threw his bag at the open locker door. "I hope you embarrass yourself out there."

Coach Peterson stood silent, considering his next move. He decided to ignore Jim's outburst. Grabbing his clipboard, he exited the locker room, and walked onto the field to prep for the start of the game.

CHAPTER 59

THE BLEACHERS WERE FILLED to capacity with a vivacious crowd eager to see the historic win. Tom arrived at the bleachers just minutes before kickoff. Someone on the fourth row recognized him and allowed him to squeeze in next to them. He quickly took his seat and surveyed the field for his son. Oddly, Jim was nowhere to be found. Sydney also entered the stadium only minutes before kickoff. She had no desire for a good seat. In fact, all she wanted that night was to blend into the sea of faces. She squeezed her way to the top corner of the bleachers and, like Tom, began searching for Jim.

Coach Peterson called his players to stand in front of the bench for some last-minute instructions. "Okay guys, let's leave it all on the field tonight. I don't have to tell you how important this game is."

He paused a moment to look into the eyes of each player. Knowing that they were going to lose that night, a thunderous pep talk seemed useless. Jim's attitude had drained his team's energy and had already sealed their fate.

"On three, guys," he said while putting his hand out into the middle of the circle. "One. Two. Three," he yelled.

"Evansville." The team monotonously responded.

The starting players took their positions on the field as the crowd stood to cheer.

Tom was deeply troubled. "Where's Jim?" He frantically scanned the bench. "Maybe Coach is saving him for the second half."

After pondering the situation for a few minutes, he quickly rose from his seat and hurried down the bleachers and walked the two hundred yards to the locker room door. He pulled it open to discover his son getting dressed back into his street clothes.

"Son, what's going on?"

Jim reactively jumped, startled to hear his father's voice. "I'm done. I'm done with this crappy school and this crappy team. I'm transferring next year. I don't care if I have to sit out a year."

"No, you're not," Tom firmly instructed.

"What?" Jim asked, surprised by his father's stern reaction.

"This is the school your mother and I agreed on. You're staying right here."

"Well, look around, dad. Mom's not here anymore, so I guess that agreement is off."

"Look at yourself. If you give in to this anger and resentment, you have lost everything you have worked for. You've got to find your faith, son."

"Faith? You want faith, huh?" Jim yelled. "Where was God that night? On vacation? Taking a nap? Answer me that! Where was God when mom needed Him most? When I needed Him most?"

Tom took a second to compose his thoughts. "Don't do this, Son. I know your mother is in the loving arms of our Savior. She's watching you and must be so upset with how you're acting. Your mother fully believed in miracles. She believed in you. And, I'm sure she wishes you would believe in those things too."

"Look, *Tom*," Jim popped off. "Don't tell me what mom is or isn't doing. In case you haven't noticed, she's gone. Poof. Vanished. You see her anywhere? Huh?"

"This selfish behavior—it's not you," Tom responded with disillusionment. "Treasure the moments you had with your mother, instead of fixating on the loss."

"You have no idea. You seem to be doing just fine. I guess you've just moved on, huh? Already scoping around for her replacement? Maybe a sweet little thing that'll keep you busy all…"

With unexpected fury, Tom grabbed Jim by the shirt collar and threw him up against the locker. Jim's merciless words had crossed the line. Tom's powerful arms firmly held onto his son and reaffirmed with authority the tough love of a father. He had reached a point of no return and moved his face close to his son's. Tom's heart was racing; he was ready to defend his eternal love from the thoughtless words of an irrational son.

Jim shrunk in fear. He was shocked by his father's reaction and the sting of the locks pressing against his back.

"Who do you think you're talking to?" Tom spewed, gritting his teeth.

He slammed Jim higher against the locker bank. "Your mother was the love of my life. She was everything to me. Every morning, I lie in bed wishing I could just end it all and join her. All I want to do is be with her again. But, I get up. I get up, because I have to. I have a responsibility to you. I know what forever means—something you've apparently chosen to forget."

Tom stared deep into his son's eyes, probing the depths of Jim's soul.

"You can question God. You can question your faith. But never, ever every question my love for your mother!" He pulled his son in closer. "You are not the man she dreamed you'd become."

With that, he let go of Jim and backed away.

Pausing for a moment to regain his composure before turning towards the door, Tom added, "I'm going out to support your team. At least one Anderson will step up tonight, when our backs are against a wall."

He left the locker room, replaying the last vision of his son standing alone with his head hung low. For a moment, Tom felt like turning around and embracing Jim with all the love he possessed. However, he understood that Jim was at a crossroads and needed to choose which path he would take. It took every ounce of self-control he had left to turn and walk out the door, leaving his confused and distraught son alone.

CHAPTER 60

THE BANG OF THE closing door startled Jim out of his stupor. Pain, anger, confusion, and resentment boiled together. Jim clenched his fists, flexed his gut, and screamed, "Why did you leave me?"

He collapsed on the bench and began to weep. Jim was lost, weak, and, most dreadfully, alone. A broken man—cut down by a sudden, unthinkable event.

"What do I do?" He cried aloud. "Where is this strength You promised? Where is the comfort?"

Bang!

A noise from the other side of the locker room stunned Jim back into reality.

"Hey, someone there?" He called out.

No response; not a sound.

"Dad, is that you?"

Again, silence was the only reply.

Jim stood up from the bench and crept around the edge of the lockers to view the other side of the room. He was embarrassed that someone might have heard the scene he and his dad had just made. He poked his head around each row of lockers. No one seemed to be in the room, so he turned back to the bench. As he approached his open locker, an unusual flash from his half zipped equipment bag caught his attention. He reached forward, unzipped the bag, and spotted the rock CD that he had thrown in there a couple of weeks back.

The entire locker room immediately filled with warmth. The feeling was so startling, Jim frantically looked around the room once again to see if someone had entered. Some type of inner peace had suddenly washed over his body. He fell to the bench, overcome with an indescribable feeling of love. It felt as if someone had picked him off the ground, literally, and embraced his fading soul. Vivid memories began to play across his mind: visions of his mother half smiling, half cringing at his choice of songs; crowds of fans clearing out as she ran down the sideline cheering him on; and late nights of her caring for his many cuts and bruises. Tears overflowed, as Jim's all-consuming resentment morphed into an immaculate change of heart.

He could think of nothing but what he'd been taught so many times as a child; that his Savior had paved the way for him to one day see his mother again. That the heavy chains of death had been lifted, through Christ's resurrection. Jim's mind became solely focused on the redemptive power of the Atonement.

"What have I done?" He whispered to himself. "How do I fix this? Help me God; tell me what to do?"

He pondered deeply, remembering the many late nights he'd

spent listening to the counsel of his mother. Tears continued to roll down his face, as he contemplated the important life lessons she had taught to him. He stared long and hard at his pregame rock CD, before whispering to himself, "Mom, if you're here, I need your help."

He heard no audible response. However, his soul burned with confidence. This feeling was coming from somewhere, there was no denying that. There was a renewed bond between mother and son, somehow, linking heaven and earth. Feeling a sudden wave of power, he arose from the bench, walked towards the stereo, and put in the CD. Music began to fill the room.

"Turn it up," the command flashed through his mind, as if the words had been whispered directly into his soul.

He briskly reached over and turned the dial to its max. A smile spread across his face, as adrenaline began to pulse through his body. He looked up at the ceiling and yelled, "Game on, mom!"

CHAPTER 61

THE FAINT SOUND OF music streamed out of the locker room and onto the field. The mood in the stadium was so dead; the faint guitar rift audibly drifted across the field and could be heard by most of the players. Bryant looked around for answers; for the source of the noise. He knew the song—it was Jim's favorite.

He looked over at Lance. "Do you hear that?"

"Yeah. What's going on?"

"I don't know."

By that time, Tom had already arrived back at his seat on the bleachers. Before long, he also heard the faint sound of rock music coming from the building. Suddenly, the volume erupted as Jim swung open both locker room doors, dressed in full uniform. The crowd roared to their feet and wildly cheered his appearance. The game immediately became irrelevant to Tom, as his eyes fixed on the movement of his son.

Jim jogged to the side of Coach Peterson, fully intending to apologize and beg for forgiveness.

"Coach?" He said in a humble tone.

Coach Peterson kept staring forward for what seemed like an eternity, before turning to Jim. "Are you warmed up?"

Jim was astonished. He'd been worried Coach Peterson would tell him to park his butt on the bench. Jim had not anticipated this kind of understanding from the coach, and he did not know how to respond.

Coach Peterson directed, "Well, hurry up. We need you out there. Go in for Pete."

Jim jogged in place for a few seconds, before hustling to the center line for the substitution. Bending over for a couple more calf stretches, Jim waited for a signal from the referee to enter the game. While waiting for the next stoppage of play, Jim surveyed the crowd and quickly spotted his dad. Tom did his best to hold back his swelling emotions, understanding the courage his son was displaying in front of his teammates and the entire Evansville student body. Jim, too, was filling with emotion. He paused a moment to reflect on his renewed love and respect for his father.

The power of the moment filled Jim's mind with clarity. He wanted to let his father know how he was feeling. Jim turned around to face him, bent his fingers into a familiar shape and strongly lifted his hand sign high into the air. The crowd roared with approval, not understanding the deeper meaning of Jim's demonstration of respect for his father.

Tom had always honored this sign of affection between Debbie and Jim, and he had never dared intrude on their special bond. This time, however, it was unmistakable: the sign was for him. His muscles shook with joy as he, for the first time in his life, lifted his hand high in the air and returned the sign of affection. A powerful rush of adrenaline ran through his body. Another huge smile flashed across Jim's face, as the whistle blew for him to enter the field.

"I feel for the other team now," Tom grinned to himself. "Go get 'em, son."

Jim sprinted to his center position and turned to glance at the crowd one more time before the restart of the game. He suddenly spotted Sydney in the top corner of the bleachers, deeply imbedded in the sea of people. She quickly looked away, trying to pretend she hadn't caught Jim's momentary glance.

"You ready?" Lance asked, arriving at Jim's side, pulling his attention back towards the game.

"Yes I am."

"Good. We're already down two. I've been wondering why you were taking so long to dress. Did you forget your mascara or something?"

Jim laughed as the two bumped fists.

On the other team, the Loyola players could also sense the change. Shades of fear were showing on their faces. The nightmare for the opposing team became a reality when, within seconds, the ball had arrived at Jim's feet. During the next fifteen minutes, the play was intense. Both sides were very aggressive, as Loyola tried to counter Evansville's new-found energy.

With only three minutes left until halftime, Evansville pushed the ball into the offensive zone. The ball rebounded off a Loyola defender and over the end line, awarding Evansville a corner kick. Jim gave a coded signal to Lance to kick the ball toward the near post. They had been practicing this play all year. Lance lowered his arm to start the play. While players on both sides began to scramble in front of the goal, Jim broke to the near post as Lance struck the ball low and hard. Jim lunged forward and volleyed the ball out of the air, over his left shoulder, and into the back of the net.

Evansville—One; Loyola—Two.

The Evansville players shouted with excitement as they ran to surround Jim with euphoric celebration. The crowd followed with an eruption of their own. Tom was throwing high-fives to everyone within reach. Jim couldn't remember the last time he had seen his dad so excited at a soccer match.

The last two minutes of the half transpired without much fanfare, bringing play to a close. Jim grabbed a water bottle and trotted back with his team to the locker room, looking back a few times to try and catch a quick glance of Sydney. The mood inside the locker room was vastly different from the last time the team was together. Players were jubilant and full of hope. Jim made his way over to the training table and grabbed a towel to wipe the sweat from his forehead. He spotted Adriel at the opposite side of the table and decided it was best to simply head in the other direction.

"Nice shot," Adriel unexpectedly shouted towards Jim.

"Thanks," he replied with a bit of confusion.

Jim quickly realized that Adriel must have swallowed an enormous amount of pride to make that first gesture of reconciliation. Jim walked over to the opposite side of the table. No words were said between the two fierce competitors—nothing needed to be said. Each young man looked directly at the other, and they shook hands as a kind of friendly accord.

Coach Peterson interrupted the halftime celebration. "All right, guys, settle down. We need two more goals. Gather round the board. We're making a few adjustments for the second half."

The coach proceeded to dictate plans that would give his players the best chance to even the score. After a much-needed recharge, the team eagerly re-entered the field to begin the second half. The visiting team's demeanor made it obvious that they just wanted the game to be over. Jim anxiously stood outside the center circle, waiting for the officiating crew to start the game. He used the delay in the action to gaze back into the upper corner of the stands to locate Sydney. He maintained his gaze until finally she couldn't continue to look away. Their eyes locked for just a moment. A part of him just wanted to forget the game, run up into the stands, and beg for her for forgiveness. However, as the whistle blew and the second half began, he knew that his opportunity to make things right with her would have to wait.

Loyola's second half game plan was obvious; they were going to mark Jim tight. His every move was shadowed by a defender—sometimes two. The play became rougher, as Loyola tried to deflate the momentum that had swung in Evansville's direction. Hard tackles and bodies were flying all over the field. The officials understood the importance of that night's game; clearly, they were going to allow the two teams to decide the winner on the field. Very few fouls were called.

Fifteen minutes into the second half, Loyola was driving toward the Evansville goal. An opposing striker took a hard shot in the direction of the upper right corner of the goal. Evansville's goalie leapt high in the air and, with arms fully extended, heroically tipped the ball off the crossbar. Adriel gathered the ball at his feet and dribbled forward for a couple of strides, before dumping the ball off to Jim, who effortlessly moved past two defenders and placed a beautiful pass just beyond Loyola's last defender. Both Bryant and the Loyola goalie streaked towards the ball. The two collided hard, causing the ball to sail just outside the left post. Bryant writhed with pain on the ground, as Jim rushed over to check on his fallen teammate.

"You okay, Bryant?"

"Yeah; just move over a bit. I've got some girls watching me tonight, and I'm looking for a little after-game sympathy, if you know what I mean."

Jim laughed and took a couple steps back while the trainer helped Bryant to his feet. As the game continued, Evansville completely controlled the flow. Nonetheless, the ball never seemed to find its way into the back of the Loyola's net. Loyola had moved their entire team back into a defensive position, as if deciding that their one-goal lead was good enough. After Jim was the recipient of another hard tackle, the referee finally blew his whistle and awarded a free kick to Evansville. Jim and Lance positioned themselves as far up field as the defensive line would allow, without placing themselves off sides. Jim, once again, had a defender draped all over him.

The defender whispered into his ear, "I heard you got a temper. Can't handle a little pressure, huh?"

Jim paused for a moment, controlling his growing anger.

The Loyola defender egged on, "Go ahead, take a swing."

Lance eyed the situation from about ten yards off. He sprinted toward Jim and yanked him away from the taunts.

"Let it go, Jim."

"I'm okay, don't worry," Jim reassured Lance.

Jim repositioned himself at the top of the goal box and thought about the defender. "You ready for me to take a swing?" He asked the Loyola defender.

At that moment, Adriel blasted the ball up the field into the middle of the box, directly in front of the goal.

Adrenaline rushed through Jim's body, as he positioned himself with the defender to his back. The ball approached, allowing Jim to softly gather it with his chest and guide it down to his feet. With the ball never touching the ground, Jim twisted his body around and struck the ball towards the goal. He crashed to the worn grass, unable to see the results of the play. However, the explosion of the Evansville student body told him all he needed to know.

Evansville—Two, Loyola—Two.

Jim rolled to his back, clinched both fists in the air, and yelled to the Loyola defender, "I warned you."

On the sideline, Coach Peterson worked to calm and refocus his team, barking directions. "Only a few minutes to go, guys. Keep the pressure on. Don't let them breathe."

Loyola quickly set the ball on the center line and pushed it up field.

A few of the Evansville players were caught off guard because they were still celebrating the score. The ball was played wide to the right, where Loyola's striker was wide open to make an easy crossing pass back in front of the goal. Their center striker got off an open shot from about fifteen yards out. Evansville's goalie lunged sideways, once again saving the season with a miraculous two-handed catch.

He quickly sprang to his feet and, with a thunderous kick, launched the ball up the field to Lance, who was sprinting at top speed. In full stride, Lance lunged forward and placed a shot toward the goal. The mass of spectators rose to their feet, only to gasp in unified frustration as the goalie dove to make the save. The ball rolled out of bounds and Evansville was awarded a corner kick. Time was running out, and it was clear that most of the players on both teams were resigned to the fact that the game would be going into overtime. But not Jim.

He positioned himself a few feet outside of the goal box, while the Loyola players scrambled to organize their entire eleven man squad into defensive positions.

"Adriel!" Jim called. "Sit on the far post."

"What?" Ariel screamed, "Coach wants me center."

Trying not to draw attention, Jim walked next to Adriel and quietly instructed, "Just trust me. Get to the far post and stay there. Don't move. I'll get it to you."

Without further question or hesitation, Adriel accepted the direction with an affirmative head nod. When the whistle blew to start play, Adriel ran to the far post, as instructed. As expected, the entire defense collapsed on Jim, who was running toward the near post.

And he was glad they did.

Lance lowered his arm, took a couple of steps toward the corner circle, and struck the ball—once again, low and hard. As the ball moved towards the near post, a mere two or three feet above the ground, Jim strung out his body and lunged both feet forward. Defenders pounced while the goalie leapt forward to cut off the impending shot. With the defense surrounding him, Jim softly flicked the ball off his right foot, tipping it a few feet over the Loyola defender's heads. The ball gently sailed along the front of the goal towards the far post, precisely where Adriel was standing, undefended.

The pass was so clean, Adriel actually had time to smile while he easily used his forehead to tap the ball into the empty net. The Evansville players took off toward their goal, as the crowd screamed with approval.

"We did it!" Adriel shrieked as he ran across the field. "We did it!"

Evansville—Three, Loyola—Two.

Jim brushed off a couple of opposing players, popped to his feet, and ran towards the rest of his team, who were surrounding Ariel.

"Way to finish." Jim yelled to Adriel in the middle of the celebration.

"Great pass." Adriel yelled in reply.

Eventually, the referee broke up the festivities and resumed play. Loyola moved the ball up the field. Their center striker in desperation blasted the ball towards Evansville's goal, but the goalie easily gathered the ball into his hands. He held the ball as long as the ref would allow, trying to run out the clock before punting the ball safely out of bounds.

Jim pleaded under his breath, "Come on ref; blow the whistle."

His petition was shortly answered as the ref pointed his arm to the center line, filled his cheeks with air, and blew the whistle to signify the end of the game.

"We won! We won!" Coach Peterson roared, running onto the field with his hands in the air.

Bryant picked up the ball and booted it high into the stands while fans stormed down the bleachers in frenzy and filled the field.

CHAPTER 62

AFTER WATCHING THE MOST exciting game he had ever witnessed, Tom was exhausted. He did not join those emptying the stands to participate in the celebration on the field. Rather, he stood on the front row of the bleachers to take it all in. Sydney had also chosen not to rush the field. She was overwhelmed by the scene—excited for the school, but still filled with a deep emptiness. During the last couple of weeks, her world had been flipped upside down, and it seemed as if those wounds would never heal. She eyed Jim, who was uncharacteristically standing about thirty yards away from his euphoric teammates. Without warning, he collapsed to his knees.

His actions seemed to go unnoticed by the raucous crowd around him. However, both Sydney and Tom saw it happen. Instinctively, Tom leaped from the stands and ran towards the field. He pushed his way through the swarm of celebrating students, until he reached his kneeling, motionless son.

Tom frantically called out, "Son; you okay?"

After a long pause, Jim looked up at his father. With a tear-stained face, Jim slowly raised his hand for assistance. Tom pulled him to his feet for a strong embrace.

"I love you, dad."

"I love you, too, son."

"I miss her so much," Jim sobbed.

"I do, too. We'll get through this together."

Sydney's attention was riveted to the moving reunion between father and son. Tears welled in her eyes. Loneliness still gripped her broken heart, and she yearned to be a part of Jim's life again. Incapable of taking another step toward him, she slowly turned to leave, making her way down the bleachers.

After offering a few more pats on his son's back, Tom released his grip. "Way to go, son. I'm so proud of you. Now, stop hanging around with your old man and go enjoy this victory with your team."

He gave Jim a gentle push towards the mob. However, the hero of the night had a different plan. Jim looked up into the stands to where Sydney had been sitting. She was gone. Panicked, he rapidly scanned the field to find his love. He spotted her slowly walking towards the exit. To catch her, he broke into the sprint of his life. As he got close, Jim tenderly grabbed Sydney's arm from behind. She turned around, clearly startled by his touch. Their eyes locked, bodies frozen as they quietly stared at each other.

"Great game, Jim."

"Thanks. I am so glad you were here to see it."

He stood motionless, captivated by the light in her eyes. Gone was the darkness that had filled his soul for so many weeks. His warm, inviting innocence had finally returned. He was utterly lost for words, so he did the next best thing. He softly reached forward, grabbed the back of her head, and pulled her close for a gentle hug.

She unconsciously tried to pull away, feeling a residual tingle of resentment for the weeks of unbearable pain she'd endured. Jim was determined not to allow her to be pushed away due to his poor treatment the past few weeks. He held her close and hugged her once more. She suddenly broke free of his grasp. Surprised, he worried that he'd overstepped. But after a few tense moments, she moved forward. With the warm touch of her hand she lowered his chin and gave him a kiss.

With the flash of her beautiful smile, she asked, "Who taught you how to kiss like that? She must have been one special girl."

The covering frost gently lifted from the blossoming bud of their affection. The fledgling sprout had fought its way through the chill of tragedy, into the warming beams of forgiveness, forever sealing its roots in a bond of unconditional love—the strongest bond. Jim pulled Sydney toward him and embraced her with all his strength, intending to hold on forever.

"I am so sorry, Sydney. I love you so much."

"It's okay. I love you, too."

Jim pulled back and looked into her eyes, "I am so sorry for the way I have been acting. I have so much I need to say to you and so much forgiveness I need to seek. I want to…"

"Jim," Sydney interrupted. "It's okay, it's over now. We can talk later. I just want to enjoy this moment with you."

Jim pulled her in for another hug. They held each other close, oblivious to the festivities taking place all around them.

After an hour, the wild fans began to disperse. Jim and the Evansville players finally found their way back to the locker room. Jim headed straight for the stereo, pressed play, and cranked the volume up once again. His famous pre-game psych CD was now the soundtrack to their post-championship celebration. The party continued with the team singing, dancing, and spraying Gatorade all over the room. Coach Peterson made several attempts, in vain, to pull the team together for a postgame recap. But, he eventually gave in and joined the celebration.

CHAPTER 63

TOM AND SYDNEY WAITED outside for well over an hour as, one-by-one, players exited the building. Jim and Lance were the last to leave.

Jim stated as he approached the pair, "Sorry, you guys must be sick of waiting."

"No, it was good talking to your dad," Sydney affirmed.

Lance broke in, "Are you coming with the team, Jim?"

"I don't think so," Jim said, putting his arms around his family. "I'm going to hang with these two."

"Alright, suit yourself. Just don't do anything I wouldn't do."

"You mean like get an "A" in econ?" Jim said with a laugh.

"You know rookie, you may just be able to replace me as the team comedian after all." Lance said with a smile. "Great to have you back."

"It's great to be back," Jim replied before Lance turned and headed for the parking lot.

Jim and Sydney made their way to Tom's car. Tom politely moved forward and opened the front door for Sydney. Before she slid inside, she gave Jim another hug and kiss. Jim looked up to see his dad smiling in approval, offering Jim an affirmative thumbs up.

Tom joked, "I think I'll pass on a kiss, son. A man hug will do just fine." Jim jumped into the back seat with a laugh.

Tom started the car for the quick drive to Turoni's for dinner. Sydney started to fiddle with the stereo buttons, moving the radio from station to station.

"What kind of music do you like, Mr. Anderson?"

Before Tom could answer, Jim interrupted, "Wait!"

Tom slammed on the brakes. "What?"

"I left my psyche CD in the locker room." Jim shouted, while opening the door to jump from the car. "I want to make sure I have it. I am going to need it for the tournament."

He trotted back to the building and opened the front door. The locker room was empty and quiet. He flipped on the lights and took a moment to ponder the evening's crazy array of emotions.

"What a night," he thought to himself before walking over to the stereo.

His finger lightly pressed the eject button, and the CD slid out of the slot. A sudden chill shot through his body. He stared at the CD in disbelief. It couldn't be—it wasn't possible. The CD partially held in the slot was not his rock CD, but the scuffed-up, pink labeled CD with the words, "After Game," barely visible on it. Mystified, Jim looked around the room, while feeling his soul once again flood with an everlasting peace. He quietly looked heavenward.

"I love you," he whispered.

Jim stared at the CD for a few more seconds, while offering a silent prayer of thanks to his Father in Heaven. He did not want the magical moment to end, but also he knew Sydney and his father were waiting outside. He gently put the CD in its case, turned out the lights, and exited the room.

"Thanks for your help tonight, mom," he whispered as he emerged from the building.

After Jim got into the car, Tom became a little concerned. "Everything alright, son? You were in there quite a while."

"Yeah, Dad, everything's going to be alright."

Sydney looked back at him, a bit perplexed as well. "Did you get your CD?"

"Yeah, I got it."

"Let's play it," she enthusiastically requested.

Jim wavered for a moment, slowly tapping the CD case with his thumb. His mother's spirit of love once again permeated his body. He felt her near, and he knew that it was time to fulfill a sacred promise he had made with his mom years before. Jim slowly lifted his arm and placed the CD in Sydney's outstretched fingers.

She looked down at the CD with confusion. "This isn't you rock-n-roll CD? I thought you…"

"I know," Jim softly stated. "It's okay, go ahead and play it."

Tom looked over at the CD and was frozen with bewilderment. When he had cleared out Debbie's car after the accident he wasn't able to find the pink CD. It was something that both he and Jim had a hard time getting over. Without the CD, it had felt like a deep part of Debbie was missing from their memories.

"Jim, how did you get…" Tom stopped mid-sentence; he didn't need to continue. A sudden feeling of peace and understanding swept over him.

He looked into the rearview mirror and could see Jim's eyes were full of water—peaceful tears of joy were running down his face. Tom didn't know what had transpired in that locker room, but he knew it was a miracle. That is all he needed to know.

Jim sat back in his seat and gazed out the window, quietly reflecting on this sacred event. He finally understood—the frailty of this mortal world could never break the love between a mother and son; that's an eternal bond. He knew without a shadow of a doubt that his mother's spirit was alive in heaven.

The quite music of Debbie's after-game CD swelled inside the spirits of everyone in the vehicle.

Jim closed his eyes, "I'm ready, mom. I'm ready."

ACKNOWLEDGMENTS

W E WOULD LIKE TO thank all those who helped bring this book to completion. The many people who read various drafts, the editors, the designers, producer, and publisher. We appreciate your support and expertise. This book would still be just a dream without your efforts.

ABOUT THE AUTHORS

DeeJay Smith:

DEEJAY IS EXCITED TO introduce his first book to readers around the world. He was raised in Arvada, Colorado where Soccer was his first love. He played soccer at a competitive level, earning a scholarship to play at Brigham Young University. DeeJay met his true love, Richelle, during his freshman year of college and lettered in soccer all four years he attended university. He was chosen by his teammates to be their Captain his senior year. Deejay and Richelle have raised five wonderful children and currently have three beautiful grandchildren.

Jeremy Smith:

JEREMY IS A FIRST-TIME author and currently lives with his wife and two children in Salinas, California. He received a undergraduate degree in Geospatial Intelligence from Brigham Young University and a graduate degree is Space Studies–Unmanned Aircraft Systems from the University of North Dakota.